A Gathering of Stories: Halloween

Praise for other Stories Rule Press anthologies

Imaginative and just a delightful read.

I absolutely LOVE this collection!!!

Other Stories Rule Press anthologies

Contents

A Gathering of Stories: Halloween

By

BONNIE ELIZABETH
C. A. ROWLAND
JOHANNA ROTHMAN
MARK POSEY
TAMI VELDURA

Stories Rule Press

The Last Dance

By Bonnie Elizabeth

THE ANTICIPATION HAD BEEN GETTING to Len for the last month. First the Snyders had put up four skeletons marching around with their children's band instruments. Unfortunately for the neighborhood none of the children were particularly good. Two kids on trumpet, one on trombone, and one on saxophone. Seeing the offending instruments in the hands of the far preferable skeleton band brought more than just smiles of happiness. Len had no doubt the closest neighbors were practically dancing with joy.

The McCallisters had then put up their giant spider climbing down the roof of their house. The wind had tried tearing it away a few days later, but Diana McCallister had fastened it down hard. Joe McCallister told everyone who would listen how proud he was of his wife.

Len's wife, Alice, would have baked Diana a cake or something, but she'd been gone for five years now. He still missed her. He missed putting up the ghosts at the door and watching her pin the old-fashioned Halloween decorations on the windows. The last year before she died, he'd gotten a garage door cover with large eyes to stare out at the kids. In the dim light it had been creepy.

Now he didn't bother. He still bought candy. Turned on the porch light and waited. Fewer kids rang the bell. Most just went from driveway to driveway or porch to porch where people sat outside with their treats. Some just left dishes of candy out. Len appreciated his recliner even if, at one time, there had been so many kids ringing the doorbell that he couldn't even put his feet up.

That was with Alice giving out candy. He'd been the runner to get more from the kitchen when the bowl started emptying out. Alice always gave a couple of pieces to each child. Had a kind word for their costume and made a fuss over the little ones. If parents were there, it was a time to quickly catch up on some gossip until impatient children pulled them away.

Len missed Alice with a physical pain. Halloween had been her favorite time of year. And she'd died two days before it had happened. Heart attack. Sudden and unexpected. The doctors said it was so massive, she wouldn't have known what hit her, her brain waves flickering out, her soul fleeing before her body had hit the floor.

Sometimes he thought her spirit still haunted the house. The hall floor would creak between the two forward bedrooms. He'd smell apple cider on the first of October, though he never heated it up and made it. Sometimes he'd make some from one of those packets and put the hot water in the microwave, but it wasn't the same. It wasn't the way Alice would have made it.

Diana McCallister, hero of the neighborhood that she was, would usually come by in October with Alice's nut and apple cookies that were always an October treat. Something different from all the chocolate and candy that happened at the end of the month. Len appreciated Diana's thoughtfulness, as did everyone else in the neighborhood.

There were rumors that the Snyder kids no longer took band classes because of some tactful thing that Diana had suggested. Alice would have known the truth of the rumor. Len had only heard bits and pieces. He subscribed to the neighborhood Facebook group but not everything was posted there. Alice had been busy and known everything.

Len leaned back in his recliner, the cushions soft and conforming perfectly to his body, and closed his eyes. Tonight was Halloween. He had a bag of candy ready for the kids. He'd gotten Mini Snickers. Those were always a treat, those and Reese's, especially when he got the regular sized singles instead of the minis. Maybe more kids would come because he'd spent more on candy. Make it worth their time to ring the bell and wait for an old man to answer.

His body relaxed as he fell into his mid-afternoon nap. He thought for a moment he smelled Alice's perfume, the Chanel Number 5 she always wore, the one splurge, she called it. Their daughter always bought it for her for Christmas and Alice would make it last the whole year. Their son would purchase kitchen items for her, things she would never use or perhaps would make Len figure them out for her.

Alice wasn't good with new electric things, though she loved puttering around in the kitchen, cooking and baking. It gave her a sense of purpose, she said.

Two days after her death, on Halloween night, Len had been dozing in the chair. His daughter and her husband were at a local hotel. His son lived just about twenty minutes away and was at home. They'd spent long days together making arrangements and finding places for the food the neighbors had all brought.

Diana McCallister, thoughtful as ever, had merely gotten him a subscription to a food delivery service and a coupon for his favorite restaurant, that used that delivery service. She'd known the other neighbors would inundate him with casseroles and platters of cheese and crackers. Her gift would see him through the long months that came later, the ones where people were slowly forgetting sorrow would still plague him, plague him forever. Len appreciated the neighbor's thoughtfulness.

Alice had liked Diana a lot. The two had been friends, trading recipes and gossip. Diana had cried nearly as hard as Len's children at the funeral. Len himself had had tears but remained appropriately stoic at the time, losing himself only at night after everyone had left him in peace.

But that night, that first Halloween after she was gone, when Len didn't even have the will to give out candy, he'd smelled the Chanel #5 right near his head. He'd opened his eyes.

Alice stood there.

"You need to give out the candy. People will think you've died, too. And then what would the children think?"

Len knew she was talking about their children, not the ones in the neighborhood. He didn't think he had candy, but looking in the cupboards, it was all there. Alice had purchased it before she'd died. Thankfully he wouldn't be left with the bags and bags she always bought. He'd give out candy to any kids brave enough to ring the bell.

There had been a lot of them. He imagined Diana Mc-Callister standing at her door telling them that they needed to go to his house, to make him feel included. It would give him something to do. It was the kind of thing she would think of.

And when it was over and he sat in his recliner again, Alice came and sat on the sofa at an angle to his chair. The sofa was her place, the long beige thing with overstuffed pillows that his kids had loved laying on, such that everyone else always had to raise their legs or tell them to move. Grumpily they would.

"You'll be fine without me for a bit," Alice said. "I mean, it's not like you're getting any younger."

Len had given her a wicked smile.

"Are you going to haunt me?" he asked.

Alice frowned at him. "Haunting sounds like something bad. I'm not haunting you. I just want you to know I'm here."

"Or I have a good imagination," Len said. He didn't believe in ghosts. He wasn't even sure he believed in the afterlife.

"There is something after," Alice assured him. "I know you were never certain."

Len opened his eyes. It was such an Alice thing to do, to see what it was he wasn't saying and then answer the question.

"I'll be here when I can. Today, the veil is thin. We can be together for a bit, before the veil strengthens again," Alice said.

"Dance with me," Len said, standing up. Maybe it had been a dare, to see if he could touch her, to feel her body against his one last time.

They'd slow danced to "Just the Way You Are," which had been a favorite of theirs when they were young. Len had found it on the music app his son had set up for Alice and she'd come to him, wrapping her arms around his neck as she'd done when they were young. She'd smiled up at him, her perfume so familiar.

Her breasts pressed against his chest, and though they were cold, they felt solid. His hand on her back felt as if it were feeling the fabric of the dress she was wearing. It was an older dress, one he hadn't seen in years. She'd worn it to their son's wedding, the chiffon just slightly scratchy against his hand. Her back was solid beneath it, though again, his hand felt a bit chilly.

They moved on to dance to other songs, talking about things and laughing as they had throughout their lives.

"I don't know if I ever told you that my mother thought you'd never make anything of yourself. She was so proud, though, when you became an electrician. She said it was a good job. A job you could be proud to do."

"Did I ever tell you my dad thought you were out of my league?" Len asked quietly, thinking back on the days when he'd been a young man not long out of high school and just starting his apprenticeship as an electrician.

"That sounds like him," Alice said. "He never gave you enough credit. You were a good father, you know."

"You were the best mother," Len had said. "I'll miss you. So will the kids."

15

"They'll get on. Losing a parent is a natural part of life," Alice said.

Len didn't say a word, remembering how Alice had moved through the passing of her mother, helping her father gather her mother's things asking what he wanted to keep and what could go. And then how she'd been nearly bedridden with grief upon the loss of her father. Was she expecting the children to relive those times?

He couldn't imagine that the loss of him would be greater than the loss of Alice.

Sometime later, Alice had begun to fade out. Her body no long felt so solid. Her voice became hollow rather than like her real voice.

"Don't go," Len had whispered. "I can't lose you again."

"I'll come back," Alice said. She'd blown him a kiss.

And she had. Each Halloween, which was why the holiday was now Len's favorite as well as Alice's. He didn't care about the candy and the children. He didn't care so much about the decorations, although using the band instruments was a genius idea on the part of the Snyders.

This would be the fifth year he'd waited for her, hoping to see her, afraid he wouldn't.

That first year after, he'd wondered if he could tell his children. The comments he'd made asking them about the afterlife assured him they would think he was crazy if he said something. Instead, while his son's wife helped him pack away things that belonged to Alice, he'd spent time hiding the dresses that she'd loved so much. He kept her wedding gown. He would have kept the blue dress, but Alice must have given that away or something before her death. She still had the peach dress she'd worn to their daughter's wedding.

He remembered that she hadn't liked it nearly as much. The style had been nice, but she thought the peach color washed her out. The blue their daughter-in-law had suggested had looked much nicer on her. He'd wondered why she would keep that dress and not the other, but Alice wasn't around to ask.

By the time the next Halloween had wandered around there were other questions and he'd never remembered to ask her about the dress.

Len opened his eyes, disappointed that Alice hadn't shown up early. She'd only come that first year before he'd passed out candy. He suspected it was because she wanted him to keep to the tradition. If she hated the way he went through the motions, she'd never said.

Instead, they'd dance each time. He tried not to think that he had only a few hours with her. He'd try to fix his mind on the way her dress felt, the way her perfume smelled, the way her voice sounded. He kept the last voicemail she'd ever left him and listened to it at least once a week, which was down from his initial hourly listen. He sprayed Chanel #5 on a handkerchief he'd found in a drawer and left it on the dresser so he'd always smell her perfume when entering the bedroom.

Those small things made him feel closer to her during the long days when she was gone across the veil, as she said, to a place he couldn't follow, at least not then. He was only seventy. She'd been barely six-three when she'd died. Far too young, everyone said.

Len hated that he was a widower. He wished sometimes to die equally young or as young as possible now that she wasn't around. But his body kept on. His family had always been long lived. His mother had cried at Alice's funeral. Now his mother was in assisted living and would probably celebrate her hundred and second birthday.

Alice's family didn't live that long. Her parents had both died in their sixties and her grandparents had died even younger. It wasn't something a person thought of when they were young and in love. At twenty, sixty seemed impossibly old, even if there was a sense that others lived longer. The twenty years between old and too young were a minor time difference to the very young.

At sixty, the years were long, and time started to squeeze into something shorter. There were things to enjoy. Life to hang on to. Loves to never be given up.

Alone at seventy, Len hoped he'd be the youngest in his family to die. His mother told him over and over again that she couldn't lose him so soon after his father. Len's father had predeceased Alice by only a handful of months. Len thought his father lucky.

His father never had to go through the trauma of losing his beloved. His mother handled things much more easily than Len, or so it seemed. Perhaps she'd cried in the privacy of her bedroom and fell apart anew each day after his death. If so, she never let on.

Len tried to put one foot in front of the other. He let the neighbors care for him in their own ways. The Snyder girl had attempted to play a jazzy tune on her saxophone. The effort had been there. The talent had not, but Len had thanked her for her thoughtfulness. He'd even sent her one of the thank you cards that he'd gotten at the funeral home to send to those who had donated money to the heart association or had sent flowers.

Rory Callison had taken Len to several baseball games. Len had enjoyed those, though he suspected the invitation was more pity than actual friendship. The two men had little in common. David Martin and he had more in common and talked about fixing things around the house. David would come and ask Len's advice about anything electrical and the two could sit and discuss options for hours.

It was a good neighborhood. His children did what they could. His daughter lived almost a hundred miles away. She called every week to check up on him. His son checked in less regularly but those might include a visit rather than a call. His grandchildren were growing up and Alice wasn't there to see them.

This year, Asa, the oldest would be a Jedi knight for Halloween. Dierdre would be a cat, again. She'd been a cat for the last three years, but she loved cats and insisted on going as one each year.

Alice would have laughed. She probably would have made cat shaped cookies just for Dierdre.

His daughter would send pictures after Halloween of what her daughter went as. She was so little that she'd probably be a pumpkin again this year. Alice hadn't ever met that grandchild. Again, Len regretted her early passing. Life just kept going and he kept trying to hold onto Alice like an anchor to keep him from being swept away with it.

Len smiled at the thought. While he looked forward to seeing his dead wife, to being with her for those few hours every single day they weren't together, he did have others in his life that made him smile. If he died, he would be with Alice, but if he lived, he had his children.

Sometimes he did think of ending it all, but he'd never had the courage. And he couldn't bear the thought of what his kids would say. The grandchildren would be old enough to understand. They'd wonder why he couldn't love them enough to stick around. Which meant he had to keep going, keep waiting for the day when death claimed him, even if it was twenty or thirty years down the road.

He wondered how he'd keep living always waiting for that one day when the veil was thin, and he'd get to see his Alice again.

The doorbell rang, the first of the evening's children. He got up and went to the door. He now put the tray, what he'd grown up calling the TV tray, though his kids informed him that wasn't the term any longer, next to the door with the dish of candy on it.

It was the young couple next door with their three-year-old. He was dressed as a blue dog of some sort.

Len made brief conversation while giving out candy. The kid barely said thank you before turning away. He looked as if he thought this whole trick or treat thing was too much of a chore, something his parents were forcing on him.

Alice would have made the child laugh or at least talk. Len didn't have her conversational grace. It was too bad she didn't show up earlier. Perhaps as a real ghost she could still give out candy. He could feel her body, after all. That meant her hands could touch candy and perhaps hold it and give it out. Her personality hadn't changed.

It would be the talk of the neighborhood if Len's dead wife gave out candy every year. The older kids would probably come by just to see her. Alice would enjoy the chatting, but it would go on later into the night and Len wouldn't have nearly as much time with her. He liked their time together and he didn't want anything to keep them from those moments. Perhaps it was selfish, but he didn't really care.

Four other kids came to the door soon after, making him get up from the recliner to answer the bell. He'd never known how many times Alice stood up, perhaps moments after sitting down, to give out candy, until the last few years. And even then, he knew, he had it easy. The single porch light and nothing else to indicate he was home meant that many kids, particularly those who came to the neighborhood from the countryside didn't bother.

He got to sit for a bit and then another bell. It was the last one for the evening. It made him sad. Len felt oddly left out, though he knew why he was being left out. He hadn't bothered with the decorations, so the kids hadn't come by.

The Snyder kids should have, but they didn't. Diane McCallister's kids usually did, and he missed them. Of course they were probably all in high school now, too old for trick or treating. The last one had come by last year, looking a bit sheepish in a black cape and fake vampire teeth, standing nearly as tall as Len.

Life was going on without Alice. It was amazing such a thing could happen. He felt as if he wanted to cry, to mourn all over again. He would have thought that two days ago, on the anniversary of her death he would have cried and mourned but it seemed that Halloween, the holiday, brought it all back to him.

It was also the day he wanted to be joyous and to spend it with her.

The scent of Chanel #5 reached him. Len smiled. She was there, or nearly so.

He stood up, looking around, ready to set the music up.

Alice walked in in the same blue dress she always wore, the one he couldn't find in her closet. He'd buried her in another dress, one she wore regularly to church, which she loved so he knew the blue wasn't the one she was buried in.

"It's been five years," she said.

"I know," Len said. "And never gets easier."

"That's because you don't let it," Alice told him. She stood a bit more distant than she usually did.

Len walked towards her. Alice held up a hand.

"What?" he asked.

"This is the last year I'll come," she said.

"Why?" Len wondered if there was some limit on the number of times she could slip through the veil. Perhaps she wouldn't come because he was going to die in the next year. He was both happy to contemplate such a thing and sad that he would miss his grandchildren growing up.

"Because I need to move on. You've held me here for five years. I've tried to help you by reminding you that I'm always with you. I'm there every time you smell Chanel #5. I'm there every time you eat a Snickerdoodle,

21

though how your mother never made those I don't know."
Alice smiled at him. "And I'm there in the faces of our children and grandchildren."

"But none of that is you. Chanel #5 can't talk to people. Snickerdoodles can't hold my hand when we go walking. And the kids and grandkids are here so seldom. I mean, the youngest one, the one you haven't met, is a hundred miles away!"

"But there are phones. Zoom. Heck we were doing that before I died," Alice reminded him. "You're the only one refusing to move on. You have to create a life for yourself. Your mother outlived me!"

"Is she going to come?" Len asked worriedly. He loved his mother but didn't need her spirit visiting him on Halloween.

Alice chuckled. Len savored the sound of her laugh, something that made him feel so joyous.

"No. She's not going to show up. You don't need her the way you feel you need me. But really, Len, you don't need me. You need to get a life. You need to spend Halloween putting up decorations. Last year, you barely decorated for Christmas. The grandkids were sad for you. The decorations are about being festive. Let yourself be festive!"

Alice looked at him so earnestly.

"But you were the one who did those things for us. I just helped. I followed your instructions. Our tree will be lopsided without you."

"Your tree will be perfectly you, Len," Alice said. "So what if it's a bit lopsided. The grandkids will love it and maybe they'll even out the ornaments so that it's less lopsided. It'll be good practice for their own homes later in life. It'll show them that you can lose someone you love and keeping living."

"I don't really want to live," Len admitted. "Not without you. Did you know the McCallister kids are no longer trick or treating? At least they didn't show up."

22

"They're past that age. Kids grow up even when you try and stop the world because I'm gone," Alice reminded him.

Len nodded.

"Can we dance? Once more?"

"The last time," Alice reminded him.

Len put on the music and held her, breathing in her perfume, aware that this would be the last time. There would be no looking forward to Halloween another year. When Alice said something, she meant it. He wanted to cry, but he didn't want their last evening together to be him crying.

When Alice started to fade and her voice became hollow, she stepped back looking at him.

"I'll see you again when it's your time. But remember to live."

Len blinked away tears but by the time his vision cleared, she was gone. He fell into the chair and sobbed. He sobbed because he was losing her again and because he'd spent five years merely waiting to see his dead wife again for a brief evening. He had to live.

The next day, when even the McCallisters weren't up, Len started putting out the home decorations Alice had for Thanksgiving. He didn't know how to cook well enough to make the dinner, but his son always invited him. He could bring over the big cornucopia tablecloth that Alice always used. They'd just had placemats last year.

In a week or so, he'd put up the old-fashioned paper turkeys Alice always hung in the windows. The house would be festive. He'd have to find the Christmas lights so he could put those out after Thanksgiving. And the tree. He needed to go shopping to buy gifts rather than just poking around online on Black Friday purchasing things off the lists his kids gave him for their kids. Alice had always added fun things. It was time he stepped up.

Len had a feeling he had a lot of years to live yet. He couldn't just sit around waiting, being the sad old man who didn't bother to decorate. Next year he'd go to the store and get one of those huge skeletons that could reach the roof. Alice had admired those but hadn't wanted to spend the money. He'd do that for her. Maybe find someone to make an apron like the ones Alice had had, a memorial to her that only he would recognize.

Smiling, Len went about his work, looking through the decorations, making his plans. He even sent a text to each of his kids. He needed to reach out more. After all, as Alice said, he'd see her in their faces and he planned to see her as much as he could, where he could.

BONNIE ELIZABETH WRITES A VARIETY of speculative fiction. In the same way, she's hopped around in a variety of different job fields. She's worked as a veterinary receptionist, cemetery administrator, and as a licensed acupuncturist. Through it all, she wrote stories.

Her novels include gothic novels, contemporary fantasy, paranormal police procedural, paranormal cozy mystery, and paranormal women's fiction. Her short stories have appeared in a number of anthologies and magazines.

She lives in Kentucky with her husband and is bossed around by her three cats. She's currently at work on a cozy fantasy novel.

She is active on Facebook on her page Bonnie Elizabeth and you can reach her through her website, https://BonnieElizabeth.com

Apart from Love

By C.A. Rowland

TYANI SMOOTHED HER BURGUNDY SILK skirt one final time as she waited to be announced. Looking over the second-floor mahogany banister, she scanned the crowd below. The room was bathed in golden light from Victorian-period gaslights, which were added for the party. Once the law firm reception area, the furniture had been removed so that the entire space resembled a London street, with life-size dollhouse-looking buildings. The effect of the lower lighting made the guests look more glamorous, even as the underlying vibration of so many supernatural beings pulsed at a furious rate.

As she stepped forward, Lt. Sherbert's voice boomed, "Jack the Ripper and victim."

Tyani stifled her laugh. The Roger, Roger, and Roger law firm Halloween celebration required all guests, human or otherwise, to be announced as their characters before descending the main staircase. The theme, Ancestors – Real or Imagined, had brought out what looked to be some creative costumes.

The three firm partners were old-school and formal at times like these. With the house full of ghosts and other paranormal creatures, no one was excused from dressing up or participating in the annual celebration.

Tyani glanced into a 17th century gilded mirror on the wall to her left and checked her headpiece. She'd created it with medallions consisting of rings of tiny pearls and aquamarine gemstones in the middle. Three were strung together to fit her forehead, with two more hanging from the sides of the embroidered area. The stones glittered in the light as she moved forward.

New paintings by old masters had been added, and the walls were navy rather than the burgundy of last year. She recognized some from when she and the three part-

ners had escaped from Eastern Europe, so many genera-
tions before. They were being hunted and she was their
ticket out, still human enough to help them gain transport
on a sailing ship.

They rewarded her with a permanent residence in the
house for as long as she wanted and a bit of immortality.

She waited as Hamlet, Bloody Mary, and Peter Rabbit
were announced. Her turn was next.

"Marie Laveau," Lt. Sherbert announced if he were
calling roll in a line of military soldiers.

He was a barrel of a figure, dressed in a khaki uniform
and cap from another time.

She stepped down the stairs, slowly so she could
search among the guests for Domingo. Surely, he would
be here.

Her headdress slipped slightly, and she adjusted it as
she took another step. It was a nod to her famous fore-
bearer, Marie Laveau, although no one but the name law
partners knew her history. And Hades, of course, would
know. The two had a long history, one she'd inherited
from Marie.

She stepped carefully, not having used the stairs all
year. Instead, portals were her preferred transportation.

The banister was smooth to the touch as she walked
down. Ahead of her, a ghost in clanging chains floated
forward. Not very original, but satisfactory.

Tyani straightened her back and left the stairs. She
spotted Domingo, her beloved, standing in the back of the
main reception room. The tallest and darkest man in the
room casually leaned against the wall. He'd come as
Shaka Zulu. Her heart started to beat faster. They were
bonded, and she often found that their minds were connected.

She wandered through the crowd.

"You're here," Tyani said. "I wasn't sure you'd be
here since I couldn't sense your presence."

"Yes, my love. I managed to stay on Hades' good side, mostly, so we have our night," Domingo said with a broad smile. "I wish it were more. Perhaps I'll win my freedom this lovely evening."

Tyani shook her head.

"Let's enjoy our time together. Hades will never allow you to leave the underworld. Not even if you win the right to ask for anything you wish."

Domingo reached forward and grabbed her, pulling Tyani into an embrace.

He whispered, "I've missed you, how you feel in my arms, how you smell so sweet."

Tyani wrapped her arms around him, not caring what anyone else thought.

"I have loved you from the day I met you. I will love you to the day we no longer exist. But now, I want to dance."

Domingo threw back his head and laughed.

He released her and took her hand, moving toward the back of the house and the dance floor set up outside. Already, several couples and a few singles were swaying to the music. Skirts swished, and swords clashed as they moved.

The band, Skeletons in Limbo, played the violin, cello, drums, and guitar. A waltz was in mid-melody when Domingo caught Tyani again and began to move in time with the beat. They'd met in Romania and vowed to dance their way across Europe. A life no longer possible but not forgotten. And for a few moments, Tyani could almost believe they were still in Romania and Domingo was free.

After dancing through several songs, Tyani begged off on another. Domingo laughed.

"I suppose you'd like a drink," he said.

She smiled. As a spirit, she and Domingo, as well as many of those in the house, could not actually consume a drink, even though they had a more solid form for the

31

party. The Rogers had instead found ways to simulate the effects of alcohol. They were fiery wisps, which combined with the makeup of the particular spirit that sent them into a fevered pitch of joy or laughter for a period of time. Once the effect wore off, another could be consumed. Having known the real sense of alcohol, it was quite similar and fun for her.

Tyani felt the heat that could only belong to Hades long before he came to stand beside her. Domingo hadn't returned with the drinks, and she wasn't sure she wanted to engage with Hades without Domingo by her side. Still, she could not be impolite to him—no one could.

"Hades. So glad you could come," Tyani said as she turned to see whether he was in character or not. Hades was the one entity that could get away without being something other than what he was. He'd settled on a royal blue velvet jacket and matching pants. A bronzer had him looking toned and glistening in the softer light. A predatory smile graced his chiseled face.

"Are you having a good time?" Hades asked as he brushed her cheek with a warm kiss.

"I am," Tyani said. "It's such a fun party, and seeing Domingo always makes me happy."

"Ah," Hades said. "Domingo. He neglected several matters I gave him today. I was almost forced to confine him to the underworld."

Tyani held her temper.

Hades had been known to use any minor infraction of his rules or neglect of his needs to prevent Domingo from attending the party in years past. As it was Domingo's one night of freedom from his sentence to the underworld, Tyani wanted nothing to interfere with their time together.

"I'm sure he was working as quickly as he could. You know we hate being separated. Domingo would no more do something intentionally that would jeopardize that than I would," she said with a smile.

"That may be true, but as I have offered before, you can always come and stay with him in the underworld," Hades said.

Tyani had considered this offer but had been warned by Persephone, Hades' wife, not to take it. As had Mr. Algernon Roger. Whether that was because Persephone viewed Tyani's presence as a threat to her marriage or that Hades might retract his agreement to let Tyani go when she desired to leave was not clear. Mr. Al had made it clear that with Hades one of the firm's most important clients, he'd not interfere if Hades chose to keep her there.

She'd been to the underworld for a short visit several times—always when Persephone was in residence for the six months out of the human year she'd agreed to stay there. She'd felt comfortable that Persephone could hold Hades to his bargain. Otherwise, she would never have visited.

"I've come a few times, and I'm sure I'll return. Domingo and I are more comfortable in the human world. We still have things to do and see here. That requires more time than one night. Is there no way you can allow Domingo to leave the underworld? Hasn't he paid enough already?"

Tyani heard the rumblings behind her as she felt Hades' temperature increase. Drinks with ice were melting. She was on dangerous ground.

"Hades. I'm so glad you are here," Sassafras said as she joined the two of them.

Sassafras wore a long, straight black wig and a native American leather sheath with hand-painted symbols.

"My mother always said we were related to famous people in Europe and the Americas. Sacagawea seemed like an excellent choice for tonight.

Tyani wanted to warn the young woman off. Sassafras had worked for Hades on a matter that took her to the underworld, but she really didn't understand yet who she was dealing with—as if any of them really did.

Hades turned, smiled, and the room quickly cooled.

"Sassafras. What an interesting choice. I knew Sacagawea and many of her tribe and the military types who treated them so disgracefully, you know. I wasn't sure if you'd be here, this being your first Halloween with the firm. It can be chaotic and crazy with the magic flowing and you being human and all," he said.

"Mr. Roger assured me I'd be quite safe. I also have a few skills, and others who are looking out for me should they be needed. But I appreciate your concern."

Hades smiled.

"You are quite welcome, my dear. Now I have a dilemma that you may be able to help with since it involves a legal agreement," he said.

Tyani wanted to disappear. She knew what was coming, and Hades was baiting a trap for Sassafras.

"A real or hypothetical problem?" Sassafras asked.

"A bit of both, I guess," Hades said. "There was an infraction concerning a contract between me and a human. The penalty was a sentence in the underworld. The human was in love with another human. So, they are separated and long to be together. I grant them that once a year. What are your thoughts on this?"

Sassafras stared at Hades for a moment before she asked, "Is the penalty forever?"

"Yes," Hades said.

"Is the penalty equivalent to the infraction?" Sassafras asked.

Tyani slowed her breath. Did Sassafras know about her situation, or was this just a theoretical question for her?

"Not exactly, but the contact was specific."

"Ah, there is the first issue. Humans don't have the same powers as supernatural beings. Did the human have the bargaining power to negotiate the deal, or was it a take-it-or-leave-it situation?"

The temperature around Hades began to heat.

"I hardly think that's relevant."

Tyani wanted to laugh. Instead, she almost sighed in relief at the sight of Domingo coming toward her while balancing four drinks in his hands.

"Domingo, you have perfect timing. I am thirsty and famished. Sassafras, this is Domingo, my plus-one," Tyani said.

Domingo handed the drinks around.

"An alcoholic beverage for Sassafras and the special spirits for the rest of us," Domingo said as he handed them around.

Hades cooled.

"There's sustenance of all kinds in the kitchen area and back yard. Young human, you should get a bit of food before drinking anything. The liquor can be strong and is sometimes mixed with magic, although these are not. Pray that you are careful in what you eat and drink. I'd be happy to help you navigate the offerings for the guests," Domingo said.

"It's best to do that early," Tyani said. "I'd love to see what the firm's chefs have come up with."

"I would like a bit of something," Sassafras said. "Hades, will you join us?"

Hades shook his head.

"Then I'll ponder our question a bit more and talk to you later," Sassafras said.

Tyani linked arms with Sassafras and guided her away. Domingo followed close behind. As soon as they were outside, Tyani said, "Do not be pulled in by Hades and his questions. It will not go well with you. Trust me. I know."

Sassafras turned to stare at Tyani.

"I don't understand."

"I know, and that's why it is dangerous. You have not dealt with Hades enough times to know his tactics. Please, for all of us, let the matter drop," Tyani said.

35

"Ladies, over here are some of the most creative appetizers you'll ever find anywhere. Allow me to tempt you with these," Domingo said with a grin.

Tyani led Sassafras to the end of the table, where they found plates and some delicacies to try. She hoped Sassafras would heed her words. It would be a success if she could avoid crossing Hades tonight.

The trio moved between groups, with Tyani introducing Sassafras to those in from Europe and other parts of the world. Domingo stayed at Tyani's side, linking with her. Tyani relaxed as friends and colleagues explained what ancestor they were costumed as.

One spirit had come as Blackbeard, and while not related to him, he had sailed under him and teased them, saying that he knew where the treasure could be found for the right price. Another came as Marie Antoinette and was the henchman who beheaded her. Unlikely, since the being was female but it was an interesting story. As the night grew longer and more and more drinks and spirits were consumed, the stories turned darker and more extravagant.

At one point, Sassafras excused herself, and Tyani watched her go. Hades was still at the party. She was sure of it. When thirty minutes had passed, and Sassafras hadn't returned, she went in search of her, whispering to Domingo a quick explanation.

Tyani squeezed through the crowd, watching for either Hades or Sassafras. Hades was usually a bit easier since she didn't need to see him to find him. His temper changed the air in ways she could track.

As she entered the front reception area, she felt Hades. Turning, she saw him heading to the group Sassafras was talking to. She watched as he said something to Sassafras, who turned and moved away from the group. Hades was drawing her out. He'd done that before. Tyani hoped she could reach the two in time.

"So, you didn't answer my question," Tyani heard Sassafras say.

"The punishment is what it is. That's not at issue," Hades said.

"I don't know about supernatural law and that specific rule, but in human law, the punishment is meant to fit the crime, so if you want my opinion, I'd need to know that," Sassafras said.

"It's not the same for supernaturals. If you violate the agreement, then the punishment is administered. In this case, the punishment was banishment to the underworld," Hades said.

Tyani tried to push forward. Sassafras was venturing into an area she shouldn't. Something or someone was holding Tyani in place, most likely shielding her. Most likely, it was Hades. Her hands shook as she tried to use them to break through. Another minute and she'd contact one of the Rogers. They would want Sassafras protected.

"What was the crime?" Sassafras asked.

"A forbidden love. The two were found together, and the punishment was to separate them. One was sent to the underworld and one to the human world for as long as they lived. Once the second one died, their spirits could not both exist in the underworld unless I allowed it. Nor could they both live in the human world without my approval," Hades said. "A sad tale but not unheard of."

Sassafras took a sip of her drink.

"That's not dissimilar from your story, is it? Persephone is only in the underworld for six months of the year, and because you are the lord of the underworld, you don't see her for the six months she is in the human world. I don't know how you can stand that," Sassafras said.

Tyani sent an urgent message to Mr. Al. If there was anything Hades was sensitive about, it was his arrangement with Persephone. She shuddered as she waited for his response.

C. A. ROWLAND

It was quick. The entire room shifted as if a heatwave had blown through. Hade's face was a mask of anger and frustration. Sassafras stepped back but seemed unflustered at the change. Tyani wasn't sure she'd have handled that as well. She was shaken to her core at what had just been said.

"How dare you question my authority. My personal life is my own and not the subject of this example. You would do well to think before you speak," Hades snarled.

Hade's anger loosened his control on the crowd, and Tyani reached Sassafras just as she was responding.

"I meant no disrespect, and if I crossed the line, I apologize. My comparison was only that often, there are lovers who are separated by forces they cannot control. The classics are full of them. Romeo and Juliet, for example, and many more. Love makes for strange actions that might never happen but for the love of two," Sassafras said.

The room cooled, and Hades considered her words.

"I don't think I was wrong, but your words give me something to consider. That's why I like working with you. You always make me think, even when I don't agree with you or don't like what you said," Hades said.

He turned and walked away.

Tyani turned to Sassafras and said, "What were you thinking? Hades can be less than rational. He's been known to send someone to the underworld on a whim."

Sassafras smiled.

"I know. I've seen him do that. But he cools down. He's been known to reconsider a position once he's thought it through. Maybe he will do that there."

Tyani was stunned. Everything in her being told her to scream and shake this young woman. What she had done was crazy. She could barely think what Mr. Al would say. He'd given Tyani specific instructions to watch over Sassafras, and instead, she'd left her open to Hade's wrath.

She needed another glass of spirits before she sent him another message.

Tyani turned and headed to the bar. She was waiting in line when Hades approached.

"Did you set her up to do that?" he asked, his hot breath flowing around her.

"Of course not. I've never discussed my situation with Domingo with her," Tyani said.

Hades reached for a glass of spirits. Tyani took hers from the bartender and sipped, glad for a moment to calm the twisting in her stomach.

"If I didn't know better, I'd say you used her so we could have another conversation about you and Domingo," he said.

Tyani drew in a quick breath. It was now or never.

"I can't say I'm sorry she did that. I did want to talk to you about that situation. Sassafras has a point. Domingo was reckless, but the young so often are. Isn't there any way you can see your way to letting him leave the underworld? Some way we can work this out?" Tyani asked, hoping she'd struck the right tone.

"No. You know the rules. And you can always visit Domingo, as you know. How would I look if I let him off? Many, many others, would want the same treatment."

Tyani's temper rose, and she could feel her ancestor's blood roaring through her veins. She'd humbled herself in a way she'd promised herself she'd never do. That ended now.

"I am amazed Persephone keeps her side of the bargain. You knew Domingo didn't know what he agreed to. You knew he thought he could work off his debt to you. You lied and cheated him."

The room's temperature began to rise.

"You dare to challenge me? After all I've done to keep him safe in the underworld? You ungrateful bitch. You aren't worthy of even dressing in costume as Marie

Laveau. She was a woman who knew her power. You are an ant, a worker bee, a tiny speck of sand. Nothing special," Hades said as he turned his back.

How dare he? Tyani straightened her back to stand tall and solid against him. He might be able to take her, but she'd put up a fight he wouldn't soon forget. She'd vowed not to use her dark power, but this was more than she could allow. Her ancestors would never stand for being treated this way, and neither would she.

"You can't talk to me that way. I've treated you with respect because you held Domingo's soul in your hands. That stops now. I'll find a way to take him from you and everything else you have," Tyani said with a low voice filled with power and anger.

Hades turned and smiled.

"There you are. I wondered what it would take to bring out the real Tyani. It's a beautiful thing. I want no war with you. Domingo is free to go if he wishes," Hades said.

Tyani shook her head. What? She needed to think. Hades never gave anything for free. Had she won simply by standing up to him? That made no sense.

"Of course, you know that if he returns to the human world, he will be human. And as a human, he will die a bit every day. Unlike you, my dear," Hades said.

Tyani swallowed hard. She and Domingo had talked many times about what they would do if Hades ever released him. The fact that he would age and she wouldn't hadn't ever come up.

"I can see you hadn't considered this. Perhaps you should be the one to talk to Domingo about this rather than me. It seems that your future together is more complicated than you realize. I have saved him from aging all these years. And you have each other for all time this way," Hades said.

"That doesn't seem fair. Isn't there some other compromise like you and Persephone have? Maybe something like Domingo living in the human world for part of the year. That would be Tyani and Domingo's decision, of course, with your, uh blessing," Sassafras said with a smile.

Tyani hadn't heard her come up but was grateful for Sassafras' input and the time it gave her to think.

"It seems you have caught me on a good night, and Domingo has also won the right to ask me a favor. He doesn't know that yet, but he was voted my most trusted assistant in the underworld, which comes with that prize. I suggest you two talk and let him tell me what he would like. It's all subject to my discretion, of course. But as you can see, I can be reasonable. I also have a soft place in my heart for tragic lovers."

Sassafras grinned.

"I knew there was still some good in you," she said.

Hades harrumphed and headed toward the front room. No doubt he'd torture some other poor soul or see what trouble he could stir up.

"Did Mr. Al tell you of my situation with Domingo?" Tyani asked.

"No," Sassafras said. "You've been teaching me to use my intuition and to follow the lines I can see around some beings. I sensed a bit of discord between Hades' remarks and the connection I could see with Domingo. Don't worry, you don't give away much, but I've been studying with you long enough to see shifts in your emotions sometimes."

Tyani's shoulders relaxed. She reached over and hugged Sassafras.

"How? You're a spirit? But you felt solid," Sassafras said.

"Halloween. One night only, which is why Domingo comes from the underworld on this night. The story is long. The Rogers saved me. They also graciously gave me

41

this night when Domingo was sent to the underworld. The offer from Hades is much more complicated than what has already been revealed."

Sassafras moved closer to Tyani.

"I am sure it can be resolved. Will Mr. Al help? Or the others? I'm not sure what I can do, but if there is anything, I will gladly assist."

Tyani's eyes filled with tears.

"So much to consider, but for now, I go to Domingo. I won't waste our time together this night. Tomorrow is soon enough for pondering the future. Go, have a fun time," Tyani said with a sad smile as she turned.

"There you are. I've been looking all over for you. I saw Hades nearby. Did you already talk to him? I thought we agreed to do it together," Domingo said.

Tyani frowned.

"I did. I suspect Hades shielded us so you wouldn't see us talking and come over," she said.

Tyani brought him up to date on the extended time they had together and the possible terms of changing his service in the underworld.

"It's a lot to think about," he said.

Tyani nodded.

"When is our answer due?" he asked.

"There's no time deadline. Let's enjoy tonight and to-morrow. We can talk this out the next day and maybe seek some help from Mr. Al or others," Tyani said.

He nodded, although he seemed distracted. Tyani be-gan making her way over to the stairs leading to her apartment.

As she moved through the crowd, Tyani heard the slap of the glove, recognizing the difference between flesh meeting flesh and leather meeting flesh. The swish of swords being drawn from their sheaths followed quickly, as did the shuffling of boots moving to make room for the fight.

She grinned. A sword fight was just the kind of distraction she and Domingo needed to slip away for their time alone. A Roger law firm party was not complete without a sword fight. While she loved seeing the swordplay skill, she'd trade seeing the duel for more time with Domingo. They had more than enough to discuss, but first, they had a night and a day to get reacquainted in other ways.

C.A. ROWLAND IS A recovering lawyer turned writer. Raised in Texas, she now calls Tennessee home – a place of history, folklore and inspiration. She's published short stories and is currently finishing the second in her amateur sleuth mystery set in Savannah, Georgia.

For more information, see https://carowland.com.

No Tricks. Only a Treat.

By Johanna Rothman

SOPHIE BARNES GRINNED WITH DELIGHT at the Arlington Boys and Girls Club's gym's total transformation. Outside, the Halloween wind gusted, swirling the remaining red, yellow, and brown leaves. Inside, at the Spooky Ball, the gym was festooned with six-foot black paper spiders and their even larger black paper webs. Two white skeletons adorned each of the two basketball hoops at either end of the gym.

The skeleton deejay at the table under the far basketball hoop swooped and swayed to the Monster Mash song. He wore a full-face mask, so she couldn't tell if he was singing the words — but she started to hum along. Who could turn down the Monster Mash?

Not Sophie.

And clearly not all the sexy and wicked witches, plus vampires and skeletons, bopping along to the song. The ball had started at seven, and now, almost nine in the evening, it was rocking.

Even with all the people, the gym still smelled a little like sweaty kids and their socks. Plus the sugary odor of sweets.

On her left, the coat rack to the side of the bleachers was full, and beyond that was a groaning table, filled with sweets from the local Arlington bakeries. She sure hoped there were some savory delights there. Just from the smell, her teeth already could feel the sugar.

Just in front of the coat rack were several boxes and bags waiting for canned goods and kids' books. She eased her bag of canned goods and books off her left shoulder and placed it with the other bags. Then, she hung up her coat and eased her small black cross-body bag over her "sweet witch" costume. While she loved what the Spooky Ball stood for — food security and books for kids who didn't have enough of either — she was not really a costume kind of girl.

The walls were filled with kids' pictures of witches, goblins, and plenty of pumpkins. And the lazy rotation of the disco ball made the pictures light up in strange ways. She suspected someone had used glow-in-the-dark paints.

She glanced down at her costume—a lightweight black scoop-neck jersey dress with long purple sleeves and a matching purple and black hat. That plus her low black heels would be good enough for tonight. She'd used her small cross-body bag for her phone and keys and small wallet.

She thought she might fit into the Ball, what with all the other witches. There were plenty of sexy witches in red, and even more scary witches with green faces and hands and crooked black hats. She wasn't so sure there was another sweet witch here, which was just fine with her. All the vampires and skeletons set the stage for the Ball very well. She thought she saw a couple of M-and-M couples, but those were too sweet, even for her.

Her best friend, Tina Davis, also the COO of the Boys and Girls Club, had begged her to come and to tell everyone she knew. Sophie had done both, even though she hadn't quite felt up to a party.

Her ex, Jake Thompson, had taken a job in Los Angeles in February. He'd said he just couldn't take any more of the Boston winter.

While she understood, she hadn't even considered going with him. As the CEO of a startup, she wasn't just responsible for herself—she was responsible to all the staff and the customers. She couldn't just up and leave. Ever since then, she'd wondered if she'd made the right decision.

She'd said—and Jake had agreed—that a long-distance relationship was not going to work. But just because they'd agreed didn't make it easy to go out with other people. This was her first party where she was even open to the idea of meeting someone to date. Her stomach grumbled, partly out of hunger, and partly out of fear. And, if she was honest with herself, out of nerves. Trick or treat—and too often, dating meant trick. Definitely not treat.

She feared she'd lost her dating mojo. But this was a great place to practice getting her mojo back. She suspected she wouldn't find anyone who could dance, so maybe she'd just start a bunch of line dances. She pasted on a smile and started to walk through the mob of sexy witches, vampires, and skeletons.

The music changed to the Ghostbusters theme. Tina, as a sexy witch in red, grabbed her and started a line dance. Sophie's smile became genuine as she threw herself into the dance.

FROM HIS PERSPECTIVE AS THE deejay, Jake Thompson surveyed the room, specifically keeping an eye on the door. He wanted to see Sophie in the very worst way. But he was the one who'd left. He was the one who'd said they should see other people.

With the dancing, the gym was a little warmer than when he'd arrived. Back then, it had felt just as if the wind whipping up Mass. Ave from Boston Harbor had infiltrated the gym. He'd left his red top hat on and his skeleton mask down for two reasons. One, he didn't want Sophie to know who he was—yet. And two, he'd been cold. The hat and the mask kept him warm.

He might need to rethink that strategy now.

He'd rented his costume—a black jacket and pants with skeleton bones painted on. His white shirt had lace

49

at the neck and cuffs. He wasn't sure normal skeletons wore lace, but what the heck? His red top hat was also decorated with lace.

Now, the heat of the dancers made the room much warmer.

He patted his jacket over his heart. Inside the jacket pocket, he had a present for Sophie. Hopefully, she would take it. A little treat, not a trick.

His stomach grumbled, reminding him he was hungry and thirsty. Since this was a Boys and Girls club, they had water bottles and fruit punch, but no alcohol at all. Must be part of the antiquated Arlington blue laws. That was fine with him. He suspected the party would stay fun, not be out of control.

He could smell the Halloween donuts, cookies, and other sweets from here. He grinned under his mask. Tonight was about having more sweetness in his life. Not so much about the snacks, but definitely about Sophie.

He'd been wrong to move to the west coast. He was still totally stuck on her. He might even have left out of fear that they had something that could be the Real Thing.

It had taken him all of a week to realize he missed Sophie. And then, only two more weeks to realize why. He was in love with her. He didn't want to date anyone else.

And because he thought he had to be a self-made man to compete with her, he'd left. What a trick he'd played on them both. Sophie was the best thing that had ever happened to him and he'd determined to find a way back to her.

So, he worked hard and surfed too little. He took dance classes so he could share in something that made her happy. And two weeks ago, he'd quit and flown back to Boston so he could be here tonight.

He had realized that being a self-made man meant something different to Sophie. It wasn't about the money to her—it was about doing things that made other people better. When he'd been in LA, he'd finally recognized that she wasn't competing with him. She only competed as the CEO with her competitors.

Well, he was here now and ready to get her back. If he could.

The lazy disco ball illuminated the door—and that's when he saw her. Somehow, she was already near the bleachers. Just in time to start dancing. If he knew anything about Sophie, it was that she would dance as soon as she could.

Next on the playlist was the Ghostbusters theme song. When it came on, Tina, the Girls and Boys Club COO—and Sophie's best friend—grabbed Sophie and started a line dance. He thought they made a nice pair—a sexy witch in red and a sweet witch in purple.

He only wanted that one sweet witch.

As all the witches, vampires, and skeletons lined up and danced, he grinned. He sure hoped the photographer was getting candid shots of the Spooky Ball. All these costumes—and dancing—made for a great party.

The dry ice fog had decreased—it was time to replace the dry ice. That meant it was also time to change places with the next deejay. He'd been here for two hours.

Now that he was ready to find Sophie, Jake felt a bead of sweat drip down his back. That sweat wasn't from the dipping and diving of his deejaying or the heat of the room—it was from nerves. Was she still stuck on him? Would she even give him a chance? It was time to find out.

The next deejay, a vampire with all-too-realistic long teeth, tapped him on the shoulder. "My turn, man. I already replaced the dry ice."

"Thanks," Jake said. "Do you need a tour of the software?"

The vampire shook his head. "Nope. I'm cool. You got the playlists in the regular place?"

"Yup." Jake paused. "Do me a favor, okay?"

"Anything, man," and the vampire smiled.

Jake tried to cover his involuntary shiver. Those teeth. "Do me a favor and stick with the Halloween rock for another hour. Then go to this playlist, okay?"

The vampire looked at the playlists. Then he smiled even more. "Trying to impress someone with a little romance?"

Jake nodded. "Wish me luck."

"You got it, man."

Jake scanned the crowd for Sophie. Ah, there she was, at the refreshment table.

PLEASANTLY WARM FROM HER DANCING, Sophie opened a bottle of water and chugged about a third of it. Then she glanced over the sweets. The cookies smelled fabulous and looked adorable.

Tucking her water under her arm, she grabbed a small white plastic plate and started to walk down the table. She took one of the orange pumpkin cookies with green icing stems. She waved it under her nose and smelled cinnamon and nutmeg, not just the light pumpkin odor. She took a bite and put the rest on her plate.

Soft and chewy, and tasted just like pumpkin pie — but without whipped cream.

She walked down and took a chocolate donut hole, and then a spinach ball of some sort. She took a bite. It was delicious, with a hint of garlic and onion. She put another on her plate and grinned to herself. The garlic would take care of the vampires.

She turned and almost bumped into a skeleton — oh, the previous deejay. She smiled and said, "Nice job with the previous set. Great music choices."

He said, "Thanks."

Her eyes widened. She thought she'd never hear that voice again. But she needed to make sure. She said, "You sound like someone I knew, Jake Thompson. But you can't be because he's on the west coast. Would you be so kind as to raise your mask?"

He took off his hat and raised his mask and smiled. "Hi, Sophie."

"Jake? You're here?"

She stopped smiling and frowned. His soft brown eyes looked the same. His face looked thinner, but paler than she expected, given that he lived in LA.

What was he doing here?

Jake got as close as he could to Sophie so he could get her attention as soon as she turned around. But before he could say anything, she turned and saw him.

She looked just the same. The light catching her deep blue eyes made them sparkle, as if she was smiling. Then she did smile. Her entire face lit with delight, and he wondered why he'd ever left.

She asked him to raise his mask.

He took off his hat and ran his fingers through his hair. Then he raised his mask and smiled at her.

She frowned. "You're here?"

He nodded.

"What are you doing here?" She shook her head. "I knew coming to this dance was a mistake."

"I wanted to talk to you," he said.

"So, talk."

A fellow skeleton jostled Jake in his quest for a bottle of water.

Jake grabbed a bottle himself and said, "Let's go outside the gym so we can talk in private."

"Fine," she said and turned to the exit.

The music turned to Thriller and a sexy witch tried to grab Jake. He shook her off, but by the time he was free, Sophie was almost to the door.

Behind her again. But this time, he didn't feel as if he was catching up. He just hoped he hadn't fallen totally behind.

SOPHIE LED JAKE TO THE next room down the hall, the dance room. With mirrors at the front and a bench at the back, there was a dark gray cabinet about waist-high just to the left of the door. It was probably someone's leftover kitchen cabinet with some kind of dark gray laminate covering. The Boys and Girls Club excelled at reusing things.

The light gray walls had large photos of famous male and female tap dancers, and the Club's dance teams. She smiled—it was a charming room, all with the focus of getting kids to dance.

There was a computer and two speakers on top of the cabinet, all locked down. She smiled. Smart. Even though this computer was a cheap model—as were the speakers—there was no sense in letting anyone just walk away with anything.

She looked around—ah, there were the two large bass speakers also, in the back corners of the room. They were heavy enough that she suspected they weren't locked down. Besides, everyone knew those speakers were for the deaf kids.

She turned and walked to the back of the room, to the four black folding chairs between the two speakers. Her heels clicked on the hardwood floor.

Someone must have cleaned this room in advance of the Ball, because it did not smell of stinky-kid feet. Instead, it smelled of wood cleaner.

She could just barely hear Thriller. Not a surprise, because she had been on the team that had tried to add more soundproofing to this room. That way, it didn't matter how loud the music was.

When the deaf kids came in here, they needed to feel the music. And with the big bass speakers, they could. That meant that even the deaf kids could learn to dance. A real taste of physical freedom for them.

She sat on the chair farthest from the door. She put her water bottle and plastic plate on the chair in front of her. Now, she was ready for Jake to speak.

"I guess I handled this wrong," he said. "I wanted to surprise you."

"You did," she said. "You couldn't have surprised me more than if you'd been a bat and had flown in from somewhere."

He chuckled. "A bat?"

She grinned at him. "Yes. A bat. Well, it would have been worse if you'd been a vampire. But I have garlic." She motioned to the spinach ball on her plate.

"Are they good?"

"Fabulous. Want one?"

He grinned and reached over to take one of hers.

She gently swatted his hand away. "Get your own. These are mine."

He stopped smiling.

She looked at his face. He looked the same, but tired and thinner. His hair was blonder, as if he'd spent more time outside, but he didn't have a tan.

"If I get some, will you wait here for me?"

She took a bite of the spinach and garlic ball and considered. She shook her head. "Not sure. I thought I just got over you. This is my first real party where I thought I'd meet more people. You know, possible date kind of people. And now you're here." She paused. "I'm very confused."

She took another bite to finish the spinach ball. It was so full of garlic, she suspected she'd smell of it shortly. That was fine with her. It would keep vampires and possibly Jake away.

"I realized LA wasn't right for me," he started. "The job was only okay. But the surfing was terrific!" He smiled.

She smiled back at him.

"But you weren't there." He stopped smiling. "I met a few people, but no one measured up to you. I really want to try us again."

She shook her head. "Not long distance. I won't do a long-distance relationship."

"That's why I quit my job and came back."

JAKE WATCHED SEVERAL EXPRESSIONS COME and go across Sophie's face. He had no idea what any of them meant. All he knew was he was here and in a place that held a lot of meaning for her.

He looked around at the spartan room. "Let me guess," he said. "This room is for dance."

"Yep."

"You spent a lot of time here?"

She nodded. "I was in every dance class you can imagine. Tap, jazz, even modern."

"Ballet?

She shook her head. "They didn't offer ballet. I learned later that they didn't offer ballet because the shoes were so expensive and growing feet outgrew ballet shoes way too fast."

"Let me guess," he said. "You've since donated enough money for kids to have ballet shoes now, from an 'anonymous' donor. Am I right?"

She looked at him, her blue eyes wide, her mouth open. She shut her mouth with an audible click and asked, "Who told you?"

He laughed. "No one. That's so you. I know you. Even though I haven't been here since February, I know you. I really want to try again."

She sat back and crossed her arms.

He leaned forward.

She pushed her chair back a smidge.

He leaned back.

She stopped moving.

He realized he was going too fast. "Let me prove it to you."

"How?" she asked.

"Let's dance," he said. "I've been taking lessons."

"Lessons?" she looked at him. "I tried to get you to take dance lessons when you were here. You wouldn't have any of it."

He pulled on his cheeks, as if rubbing his beard. "Yeah, well. I heard dancing is a great way to pick up women."

She laughed, the first laugh he'd heard from her tonight. "Did you pick any women up with your dancing?"

"Not really," he said. "First, I'm not a disaster on the dance floor, but I'm not great. I did learn to lead a little. And I stopped looking at my feet."

She smiled again. "All good things."

"Yeah," he said. "But there was a problem with all of my dance partners."

"What was that?" she asked. "They couldn't all have been bad dancers."

Jake shook his head. "No, they were great dancers. But they weren't you."

Sophie shook her head. "See, that's the problem. We were only together for six months. Then you left. Now, you were in LA for eight months and you're back. How can I know you'll stick around for the long term?"

"Are there any guarantees in life?"

She shook her head. "No. No guarantees about anything."

He leaned over and gently took her hand. It was cold, which didn't make sense since she'd just been dancing in the auditorium. "Dance with me? Please?" He grinned. "I learned how to use this system and made a playlist just for us."

SOPHIE COULD NOT BELIEVE JAKE was holding her hand. What was wrong with her? She hadn't gotten this far by being a coward. She stood up and said, "Yes. Let's dance."

He strode over to the computer and started the music. It was *Love Potion Number 9.*

She laughed out loud. That was Jake's sense of humor.

He rumba'd over to her, swiveling his hips as he danced over. He stopped directly in front of her and extended his arms so she could get into dance position. He said, "I have a confession. I only know how to rumba and foxtrot. My swing is uneven and my waltz isn't smooth enough. But I got somewhere on my rumba and foxtrot."

She laughed. He was as clear-eyed as ever about his capabilities. "Then we'll rumba to this one."

He smiled and drew her into dance position. He closed his eyes.

58

"Are you counting?" she asked.

"Yes! Shush. I'm not that good yet."

She giggled, and her shoulders went up and down. Then she took a deep breath in and firmed her arms.

He started to lead.

A nice firm lead, so she knew what to do. Every time the chorus came around, he turned her in a lovely swirl. She hadn't danced with anyone in way too long. He felt good. And he smelled good. She sniffed him. Just clean man, with his own scent.

She was happy, happy for the first time in a long time. The song ended earlier than she expected.

He said, "I didn't even know you'd be a witch tonight. But this is perfect."

That's when Frank Sinatra came on with Witchcraft. And he swooped her into a foxtrot.

He was a better dancer than he'd let on.

JAKE HAD NO IDEA DANCING with Sophie would be this much fun. She fit perfectly—no, they fit perfectly together. He led, she followed.

He suspected that if she let him back into her life, dancing would be the only time she would follow him—and that was totally fine with him.

She smiled, her head canted a little to her left.

His heart beat in time with the music. Maybe he'd make his pitch to her again after the song ended.

He led her around the room, alternating turns to the left and then to the right.

When the song ended, he heard clapping.

There was Tina standing at the door, clapping, her eyes crinkling at the corners. "There's more dancing next door, you know." She strode over and stopped the music. "Come back to the party."

He let Sophie go, feeling uncertain, his stomach churning. He wasn't done yet.

"This was lovely," Sophie said. "But—"

He laid his finger across her lips. "Please don't say no. Please say you'll give me a chance." He took his finger away and practically held his breath.

"A chance. But you already broke my heart once. I can't take another time."

"I won't break your heart again. I promise."

"No guarantees," she said. "Remember, there are no guarantees."

"But there are promises," he said and reached into his jacket pocket. He pulled out a white envelope. "I think this is a promise you'll enjoy." He gave her the white envelope. "This isn't a trick. It's a treat."

WHEN TINA INTERRUPTED THEIR DANCING, Sophie wasn't sure what to think. The music had carried her away—probably too far away. Jake had great form, if a limited number of steps.

And his music choices charmed her.

Too bad he hadn't taken dance classes with her last year, when she'd asked him to.

But that was last year and now he was asking her to take a chance on him again. On Halloween.

The white envelope crackled between her fingers. She opened it and read the piece of paper. It was a payment for ten dance classes for Jake Thompson and Sophie Barnes. Ten classes.

She looked up at him, feeling her face stretch into a huge smile. "This *is* a treat! Thank you!" She felt surer of them now than she had just a minute or two before.

"When do you want to start?" he asked, smiling back at her.

"Monday."

"I'll make the appointment," he said. "Now, can we return to the Ball?"

"Yes," she said and slipped her arm through his.

JOHANNA ROTHMAN

A MULTI-GENRE FICTION WRITER, Johanna Rothman writes about intelligent people who create — or encounter trouble. Regardless of how they find themselves in trouble, these characters find solutions — often in imaginative ways. In addition to her short story collections, she has published short stories in Pulphouse Fiction Magazine, Fiction River, and Holiday Spectaculars.

An award-winning author of twenty nonfiction books about managing product development, Johanna incorporates humor — not just practicality — into her nonfiction. All because life is too short to take *too* seriously.

See her newsletters and all her writing at https://jrothman.com and https://createadaptablelife.com.

Song for a Ghost

By M.D. Posey

Ghostly Reunion

LILLIAN THOMPSON CARRIED THE FINAL box out to her Cayenne and crammed it into the back seat. It really was amazing how much crap could accumulate in five years. This last box was filled with flats she didn't wear anymore. Jonathon had preferred high heels.

Why had she always catered to what he wanted? Like this Porsche. She'd let him talk her into buying the damn thing, now she was stuck making the hefty payments on her own with no job, no home, and now, no Jonathon.

As her first act of independence, she'd dug the locket that Daniel had given her out of the back of her jewelry box. When the car accident had taken him from her, she'd pledged never to take it off.

Jonathon had never let her wear it. Now he could go fuck himself. The SOB never even had the decency to break up face-to-face.

A text.

He'd sent her a text.

Been seeing someone else and it's working pretty well. Have a nice life.

A nice life? After five years, she didn't even know where she was going to go. This was not what she'd pictured when she'd moved from being widowed to dating again.

"Lily?"

Her landlord. She realized she'd been standing there with her hand on the open door for too long. She clicked the back door on the Cayenne shut and turned to face him. He'd always been a decent sort. They were parting on good terms.

He smiled when their eyes met. "Marjorie made you a care package for the drive." He handed over the Tupperware container and she pulled the lid up. Tuna fish sandwiches and chocolate chip cookies.

"Thank your wife for me, Mr. Samuelson. And thank you for being so good to us... me." She felt the emotions welling up and tamped them down. Hard.

"Oh! These came, too. They must have slipped through the postal notice." He held a handful of envelopes out to her.

She took them from him, put them on top of the Tupperware container and set them all on the passenger seat next to the bags of Halloween candy.

Mr. Samuelson patted her on the hand. "You take care, now, Lily. And drive safe. The snow's going to come soon. Next few days, most likely before Halloween."

Driving safe she could do. But where the hell was she going?

Two hours and one interstate exit later, Lily pulled into a service plaza. She had to pee and she was hungry. Besides, she needed gas.

Once she'd filled up, used the washroom and bought herself a Red Bull, she pulled to the side of the parking lot and ate one of the tuna fish sandwiches while sorting through the mail.

Most of it was the usual crap but one letter at the bottom of the stack intrigued her. She held it up as she chewed on her sandwich. It was from Henderson, Landers and Flynn: Attorneys at Law. The postmark said Portland, Maine.

"Be just my luck, I'm being sued," Lily muttered and took another bite of her sandwich.

As it turned out, she was not being sued. If she could

appear in the offices of Henderson, Landers and Flynn and prove she was the Lillian Regina Thompson born to Richard Thompson and Catherine Thompson (nee Hughes), her uncle, Craig Thompson, had left her an inheritance.

She had no knowledge of an Uncle Craig Thompson. She'd certainly never met him. She hoped it wasn't some sort of scam. But, she had nowhere else to go and nothing else to do, and Portland was only a couple hundred miles away.

"It's a sign. It's got to be." She closed her eyes and put her hand on her chest. "Take it on faith, Lily."

She wolfed down the rest of her sandwich, had a couple mouthfuls of Red Bull and snatched a couple cookies out of the container before yanking the Cayenne into gear and pulling back onto the interstate.

Portland, here I come!

AS IT TURNED OUT, HER long-lost, never-before-met Uncle Craig Thompson had been very wealthy and left her his estate home in a town called Preamble.

Strange name for a town but what did she care? An estate home! A mansion, more-or-less. Just what the doctor ordered. Somewhere quiet and out of the way to live and lick her wounds.

Lily's heart soared as she neared the quaint little New England town of Preamble. The trees – reds, yellows and oranges – was breathtaking. She had stopped a couple times to marvel at the view and take pictures. The entire place was like a postcard. When she rounded the bend and the town proper came into view, she actually sighed.

67

It had a "Welcome to Preamble" sign at the edge of town. A gas station, a grocery store and a diner called "Mona's" stood together on one side of the road. It was nearly dinnertime. Judging from all the cars out front, the place was packed. She parked at the diner and hurried inside.

It was as if she'd stepped back in time to the 1950s. The diner still had speckled formica tabletops with wide chrome edges and dark red Naugahyde bench seats. In front of the lunch counter, a row of swiveling stools screwed to the floor with the same red Naugahyde and chrome edges. It wouldn't have surprised her if the wait-resses wore cardigans and poodle skirts and roller skated from table to table while Yakety Yak played on the jukebox.

The entire place went quiet when she walked in and sat at the lunch counter.

"Welcome to Preamble," the waitress said as she sauntered over and set the one-page laminated menu down in front of Lily. She pronounced the name of the town *Preem-bull* with a thick New England accent and wore neither cardigan nor poodle skirt. She stood in front of Lily in a t-shirt, apron and jeans, one hand braced on the edge of the counter, and waited for Lily's order.

Lily could feel everyone watching her as she quickly scanned the menu. "Can I have bacon, eggs, hashbrowns and toast with a cup of black coffee, please?" She held the menu out to the waitress.

The woman didn't even blink. "Only serve breakfast in the mornin'."

Lily pursed her lips. "Fine. A cheese burger and fries. Still want the black coffee, though."

The woman took the menu and wandered away.

"Don't worry about Marlene. If you're around here long enough, you'll learn to ignore her. She's as grumpy as the day is long." The older gentleman two stools away gave her a friendly smile. His cardigan looked brand new and went perfectly with his grey, receding hairline. He also had a thick New England accent.

"Thanks, I'll keep that in mind." Lily smiled back. "What makes you think I'll be here that long?"

He shook his head, rueful. "Educated guess. Preamble's too far off the beaten path. We don't get many outsiders here."

"You make it sound like it's one of those towns like in the movies – where they shun strangers because there's a secret no one's supposed to talk about."

He chuckled. "It's not that bad."

"You wouldn't happen to know where I could find Preamble Real Estate, would you?"

Marlene set Lily's coffee down in front of her as the man said, "I might, yes." He held his hand out to her. "Paul Bartlett. I'm the town real estate agent."

Lily brightened and shook his hand. "Mr. Bartlett, my name's Lily Thompson. I'm here about –"

He held his hand up to stop her with a glance at Marlene, leaning against the back bar, arms crossed. "We'll talk at my office just across the street after you eat." He stood and tossed a twenty dollar bill on the counter. "If we talk about it in here, the whole town will know about it by the end of the day. Have the peach pie for dessert."

IT WAS AFTER HOURS WHEN Lily headed across the street to the Preamble Real Estate office. Paul Bartlett met her at the door and let her in, locking it again behind her. "So you're Craig's niece, hm?"

"I guess so, yes. Until I got that letter from his lawyers, I didn't know he existed."

"He did mention he'd been estranged from the family. Maybe this is his way of making amends?"

Lily nodded. "Could be, I suppose. I'm not aware of any amends that need to be made."

"He tried to sell the old place for nearly a year before he died. Never got any takers. Plenty of tire kickers but, for some reason, none of them felt comfortable on the estate. Even had one couple sign the papers and move in. Two days later, they used the thirty day reversion clause. Couldn't get out of there fast enough."

Lily frowned. "What was their problem?"

Bartlett shook his head. "Never did say. And I haven't seen them since."

Lily shrugged. "Well, it's mine now. I guess I'll have to make the estate work."

Bartlett cringed. "Fair warning: estate might be a bit generous."

"Why's that?"

He leaned back and grabbed a set of keys from the board behind his desk. "Let's head out there and see what you think of your new place."

Lily followed Bartlett in his Lincoln Continental through the streets of Preamble.

"Preem-bull," Lily reminded herself.

Two miles out of town, they made a right-hand turn and then an immediate left into what looked like a trail through the bush. Grasses and shrubs had overgrown and obscured the tire tracks. They weaved through the trees for a quarter of a mile. They rounded a bend and the estate home came into view. They stopped in the roundabout in front of the house and got out of their cars.

Lily looked up at the spires at the front of the house. Bartlett hadn't been entirely wrong about the house but "estate" was not incorrect, either. The grand old house needed a generous portion of TLC. The wraparound front porch would be a beautiful place to spend a summer's evening once it was repaired and painted. The ginger-bread moldings and railings suited the house perfectly.

Bartlett stepped up to the front door. "Watch that third step," he cautioned as Lily moved to join him. He unlocked the front door, shoved it open and stepped aside to allow Lily to enter. "Welcome to your new home, Miss Thompson."

"Please, it's Lily." She took the keys from his outstretched hand as she stepped over the threshold.

"Alright. Lily. I'll come check on you in a couple days."

She watched over her shoulder as he pulled the door shut from outside. Moments later, his Lincoln started and drove quickly away.

Where's he going in such a hurry?

She scanned the entrance and strolled deeper into the house. The old Victorian needed as much love on the inside as it did on the outside. Peeling wallpaper, scuffed up hardwood floors, and dust-covered sheets over all the furniture would make it quite a project to restore. Lily's eyes grew bright as she wandered the main floor, imagining the possibilities.

Large paintings hung on nearly every wall, all signed by the same artist. Most of them were landscapes of one vista or another. The only one that wasn't a landscape was a portrait of a man and a woman that hung on the staircase wall. They looked happy and very much in love.

She ascended the staircase directly opposite the front door. Several of the treads creaked, one was outright broken, just like the third step outside. From the landing at the top of the stairs, she could see all the dust and grime on the crystals of the chandelier over the foyer.

The chandelier flickered and then died, as a cold breeze blew through the foyer. For a moment, she could see her breath in the air. She furrowed her brow and glanced at the front door to check it was closed.

Something brushed by her neck. Lily screamed.

She whirled and glanced around the landing. No one was there. Her locket thumped against her skin and when she looked down, she was surprised to find the locket open. She snapped it shut.

When the chandelier popped on again, she thought she heard soft hurried footsteps, downstairs.

"Is someone there?" she called, hand on her chest. "Hello?"

Silence. Then the furnace surged to life with a *tick tick tick*. It almost sounded like running feet.

She shrugged. "Spooky old house is playing tricks on me."

She descended the staircase without inspecting the bedrooms. Though it was still early, she had a Porsche full of possessions to bring in before it got too dark. It was nearly the end of October, after all. First order of business in the morning would be to open all the windows, pull the dust covers and see just what she had. Then she could figure out where to start.

She glanced into the parlor from the bottom of the staircase and smiled as what was obviously a grand piano under the dust covers caught her attention. She hadn't played in years. Not since Daniel had died.

Daniel. She still missed him terribly. What fun they'd had. He would have loved this place.

He always used to tease her, call her the blind pianist. She'd often find herself carried away by the music and close her eyes as she played.

Her smile grew wider as she approached the piano and tugged the dusty sheet to the floor.

She ran her fingers over the old Steinway affectionately. The lid being down would have stopped dust building in the piano's interior.

Lily lifted the fallboard and absently tickled a couple of the keys.

Lily!
She whirled around.
No one was there.

THE NEXT MORNING, LILY WOKE refreshed but famished. She decided that the first order of business before opening up the old Victorian would be breakfast. Since there was no food in the house, that meant a trip into town.

She made sure she was presentable for when she walked into Mona's and all eyes were on her by giving herself a quick once-over in the mirror.

Lily!

This time, she scanned the reflection of the room in the mirror. When she saw nothing out of the ordinary, she turned and scanned the room once more and shook her head.

By the time she had driven to Mona's, she'd convinced herself that it must be her imagination.

Mona's was as busy this morning as it had been yesterday. Once again, all conversation died when Lily stepped inside. She gave the roomful of people a quick smile and seated herself on the only empty stool at the counter, the one farthest to the right.

The same sour-faced waitress slapped a menu on the counter in front of her. Lily met the waitress's scowl with a smile. "Bacon, scrambled eggs, toast, hash browns and coffee, please."

The waitress scowled at her, snapped the menu off the counter and stalked away.

Lily shook her head. "They really don't do well with strangers in this town."

The old woman sitting next to Lily smiled. "No, they sure don't." Her New England accent was even stronger than the waitress's. She patted Lily's hand. "Don't you pay no never mind to Marlene. She don't even like herself."

Marlene returned with Lily's coffee, plunked it on the counter in front of Lily and stalked off.

"How was your first night in that new place of yours?" the old woman asked.

"How did you know—?"

"Gonna have to get used to that, Lily." The old woman grinned ruefully and shook her head. "Small town. Everybody knows everybody else's business."

"I see," Lily said. "Then you'd be able to tell me about my Uncle Craig."

The old woman pursed her lips. "Nice enough sort, he was. Always had a smile and a kind word, even for Marlene."

They both chuckled.

"Kept mostly to himself. Never married, as far as I know. No kids, neither."

"That must be why he left the estate to me."

"I reckon you got that right. Though he did try to sell it for quite a spell."

"So I heard." Lily sipped her coffee. "Any idea why he wasn't able to find any takers?"

The man seated on the other side of the old woman leaned forward and caught Lily's gaze. "Way I hear it, place is haunted. Won't let no one live there in peace."

Lily grasped her locket. "Haunted...?"

"Emmett, hush. You'll frighten the poor girl half to death," the old woman said, then she patted Lily's hand again. "It ain't no never mind, Lily. It's a perfectly fine ol' house. The moans and groans is just the wind in the willows. Nothin' more."

Emmett leaned forward again. "That ain't the way I heard it."

74

"How did you hear it?" Lily asked.

"Old man Caldwell, the artist that built the place, I heard both him and his wife died there. Right in the house. Under *mysterious circumstances*." Emmett put air quotes around the last two words.

"Emmett," the old woman chided.

"Mysterious circumstances?" Lily leaned forward to meet Emmett's gaze.

Emmett nodded. "They was both found dead in the parlor. Old man Caldwell was in the rockin' chair and the old lady was at the piano."

"She died sitting at the piano?"

"Hands was still on the keys."

"Emmett," the old woman chastised him, "you weren't even born when that happened."

Emmett ignored the old woman. "Ever since, their ghosts keep the place safe. You won't get a moment's peace livin' there."

JUST AS SHE'D DECIDED, WHEN Lily got home, she opened up the entire house. She started upstairs, propped open every creaky door and pried open every sticky window. Let the place air out. Got a breeze wafting through the house.

She also pulled off as many of the covering sheets as she could on the way through. By the time she returned downstairs, Lily had an armload of dusty sheets. She'd get the rest on the next pass through, after she'd opened up the main floor as well.

She dumped the sheets at the bottom of the stairs and started her trek through the main floor. She wedged open the front and back doors and latched the screen doors in

75

place. Then she made a circuit around the main floor, throwing open every window she could.

When she stepped into the parlor, she stopped in her tracks. The piano lid was up on the long prop.

She could have sworn it had been closed yesterday.

After she opened the parlor window, she heard the rustle of paper as the breeze swept through the room. She glanced over her shoulder in time to see two pieces of sheet music waft to the floor.

Lily frowned. She didn't remember seeing sheet music in here before.

Curious, she snatched the papers off the floor and set them on the piano's music rack. She sat on the stool and peered at them. The arrangement looked familiar, though there was no title. Just the notes.

She quickly centered herself at the keyboard, readied her hands and played the first few notes, before she yanked her hands back in shock. Her heart ached. She lifted her right hand to her locket and rubbed her fingers over it.

It was the first song she'd ever played for Daniel. The one he had always liked her to play for him.

Lily!

She snapped her head toward the front door, where the sound seemed to have come from. "Whoever you are, if this is your idea of a joke, it isn't funny!"

Lily shoved the stool with the backs of her legs as she stood. The stool's feet scraped across the floorboards with a loud squawk. She stalked toward the front foyer, unsure of what she would do when she found whoever was doing this.

Lily!

Now it was from behind her, in the parlor.

She halted and glanced over her shoulder. Was there more than one of them?

Lily!

76

Now ahead of her, across the foyer, in the dining room.

As she turned her head to look toward the dining room, she caught a glimpse of herself in the mirror on the stairway wall and what she saw made her blood run cold. Or rather, what she thought she saw, just for a second.

Had that been Daniel behind her?

Surely not. That's crazy, isn't it?

She felt silly but she turned and checked behind her. Daniel could no more be behind her than he could be standing in front of her.

"Knock, knock!"

Lily almost jumped through the roof as Paul Bartlett peered through the latched screen door at her.

"Lily? Everything okay?"

She placed her hand on her chest, the fingers just skimming the locket. "Of course, Paul. Everything's fine."

"Can I come in?"

"Certainly, yes. I'm sorry. It's been a long day of unpacking." She unlatched the door and stood back so he could come in.

His gaze fell on the stack of boxes in the foyer. "Long day of unpacking, huh?"

Lily looked at the boxes and nodded. "Well, it will be, yes. What can I do for you, Paul?"

He spread his arms wide. "I just came to see how you were settling in. Always thought a realtor's job shouldn't end once the keys have been turned over." He held up a brown paper bag. "I brought some of the apple-cinnamon muffins my wife made this morning. Thought we could have coffee, and I could give you the lay of the land as far as the people in town go."

"Having Mona's entire place go quiet when I walk in, I think that'd be a good idea. Come on back to the kitchen." As she strode across the foyer, she glanced once again at the mirror. Only her own reflection looked back at her.

Once Paul left and Lily got to her unpacking, it was indeed, a long day. She brooded about the whispers of her name and the glimpse of Daniel in the mirror. By the time she crawled into bed, she was exhausted. Although she didn't believe she'd sleep, she was asleep almost immediately.

It was dark. Lily could hardly make out her surroundings. Trees maybe. Whatever they were, they stretched toward the sky and swayed in the breeze. It didn't seem familiar at all as she wandered among them, searching for she didn't know what.

Lily!

"I'm here, Daniel!"

Lily started searching faster. Running through the trees, even though she couldn't see where she was going. She just followed the path.

Lily!

"I'm coming, Daniel! Where are you?"

Lily!

Some sort of building came into view ahead of her. It appeared to be an apartment building of some kind.

Lily! It was less of a whisper and more of a breathy voice now.

Lily plunged inside the building, found a hallway to the left and right and stairs in front of her. She rushed down the passage to the left, throwing open doors.

Lily! It had gone back to a whisper. Wrong way.

She turned and dashed into the other corridor. Even before she opened the first door, the whisper came again.

Lily!

She hurried to the stairs and started up.

Lily! The breathy voice was back.

She sprinted up the stairs, two at a time.

Lily!

Across the landing and up the next set.

Lily!

And the next set. Finally, to the top where Daniel stood, his hands cupped to his mouth like he was shouting. Lily dashed toward him, arms open wide. He vanished just as she got to him. She stumbled –

Lily jolted awake and sat up.

Lily!

The same breathy voice as in her dream!

She tossed the covers back and swung her legs over the edge of the mattress. The balls of her feet rested on the floor, her hands clasped the edge of the mattress. She held her breath and tried to make the breathy voice call her again.

Had she imagined it?

Was it just a remnant of her dream?

She waited in the darkness and the silence. After a few minutes, her head began to droop forward.

Lily!

She jerked her head up and listened again.

Lily!

She stood, groggy, and shuffled across the bedroom and into the upstairs hallway. Her arms hung loosely at her sides.

Lily!

This time it was less breathy, clearer.

Lily trundled to the top of the stairs and shambled down them like the half-awake woman she was.

Lily! A full-throated voice this time.

When she came to the mirror where she thought she'd glimpsed him earlier, her hands flew to cover her mouth and she blinked back the tears that threatened to overflow.

Daniel gazed out of the mirror at her, a wide smile on his face. "Lily."

"Daniel? Is that really you? How is this possible?"

He continued to smile at her. "Lily."

"Daniel, what's going on? How are you here?"

He glanced over his shoulder and when he turned back to her, his face fell. "Help me."

And he was gone.

FOR THE REST OF THE day, every time Lily walked past that mirror in the foyer, she peered into it, hoping to catch even a glimpse of Daniel.

No luck.

She wondered if she'd imagined the whole thing. Maybe it had been some sort of sleep-walking episode.

That night, it happened again, just as she was dozing off.

Lily!

She swept the covers off of her and hurried down the stairs to the mirror and, sure enough, Daniel was waiting for her.

"Daniel, where have you been?"

"I've been right here."

Lily shook her head. "I've been looking in this mirror for you all day. This is the first time I've seen you."

"I can't explain it. I've seen you look in this mirror many times today. I've always shouted, but you didn't hear me. Maybe it works better at night?" He shrugged.

"How did you get in there?"

"After I died, I found myself anchored to your locket with the picture of us inside. I think it was because of unfinished business—I never got to say goodbye to my true love."

Lily touched the locket at her throat as she felt the old sadness loom.

"Something about this strange, old house drew me out of the locket and into the house's ethereal plane. At least, I think it was the house."

Lily frowned. "What else could it be?"

"I overheard the Caldwells. They've grown bitter over the years, trapped here with no end in sight."

"The Caldwells? You mean the artist and his wife? They're here, too?"

Daniel nodded. "There's a one-week window where the house's ethereal plane and its real-world plane line up. But no one's ever managed to open that window."

"When is that week?"

"The last seven days of October. It ends at midnight on Halloween, if you can believe that."

"I wouldn't have believed I'd ever speak to you again, Daniel. So, I can believe that."

"There's one other hitch. With all the spirits they've encountered in the house, they've set a curse. If they can't leave, none of us can, either."

"Us?"

Daniel nodded. "There are fifteen other spirits here, trapped by the Caldwell's curse."

"Is there a way to break the curse?"

"I don't know. If it truly is 'If we can't leave, neither can anyone else,' it seems to me we have to figure out how to break their attachment to the house. There's got to be some object they're tied to."

Lily yawned. "Okay, in the morning, I'll have a look through all the nooks and crannies and see what I can find."

"Marvelous. Sleep well, my love."

My love.

Lily glowed with that phrase all the way to bed.

THE NEXT MORNING, LILY WANDERED through her new home. Slowly. She let her gaze roam over all the objects in each room that had been here when she took possession of the house.

Most of it was bigger items. Sofas, end tables and armchairs. The kitchen table and chairs. And, of course, the piano. Those were on the main floor, in the public areas.

Lily checked upstairs but apart from beds and dressers, there wasn't much. In the attic were dusty old boxes holding assorted crap.

None of it seemed to fit the bill as a potential spirit anchor. Everything in the house was too generic. It seemed to Lily that whatever the object, it would be something that was emotionally significant to both the Caldwells.

After all, the locket Daniel had originally been tied to was something he had given her. She kept her favorite picture of the two of them inside it. And she wasn't sure, but she thought the locket had belonged to Daniel's grandmother.

By the end of the day, she was exhausted, having made several laps of the house from top to bottom. Despite that, she didn't go to bed. She pulled a chair up in front of the mirror and waited.

Lily!

She jolted awake, still in the chair. But there was Daniel, looking out of the mirror at her.

"Hello, my love," he said, the smile reaching his eyes.

Lily grinned. "I've spent the whole day searching this house."

"Any luck?" he asked.

"There's very little that would have sentimental value." Lily's gaze wandered the foyer while she tried to recall anything she may have overlooked. "Hang on," she said after a moment, "he was an artist, wasn't he?"

"I believe so, yes. And she was a musician."

"The one that painted all these paintings." She swept her hand around and then pointed at the portrait of the two people on the wall. "Is that them?"

Daniel peered at the reflected painting on his side of the mirror. "It is."

Pensive, Lily caught Daniel's gaze through the mirror. "Every other painting in the place is a landscape."

Daniel brightened visibly. "That's got to be it. Well done, my love."

As effusive as Daniel's praise felt, Lily wasn't quite convinced. "Let's not jump the gun, Daniel." She headed toward the painting, intent on pulling it from the wall.

Leave it alone!

Daniel glanced over his shoulder as crashing sounded from the parlor.

Even as she turned to look, she saw Daniel move across the mirror. There was also a mirror in the parlor. She was sure that's where he was heading.

She rushed into the parlor and found the piano and its bench in a shambles. The long prop had been knocked aside, dropping the lid violently on the case, the fallboard now covered the keys, and the piano's bench had been tipped over, spilling the contents all over the floor.

Lily stood with her mouth open in disbelief.

"What was that you said about jumping the gun?" Daniel teased.

Lily raised her eyebrows. "That painting got quite the reaction, no doubt."

"So that's got to be it, right?"

"It certainly seems that way." Lily scanned the parlor, including the antique wall clock that showed it was now past midnight.

"So what do we do now?"

Lily glanced at Daniel in the mirror and stifled a yawn. "I don't know about you, but I'm hungry. You going to be here when I get back from the kitchen? We have

83

a lot of catching up to do. Besides, we have to figure out how to free the Caldwells."

It was a long and wonderful night that went by much too quickly.

In the daylight, the parlor looked even worse.

Lily stood in the parlor entrance, hands on her hips. "Don't know why you had to make such a mess," she told the room. "I wasn't going to hurt your precious painting. But I think it's the key to setting you free."

She felt silly standing there, talking to the air. But she wanted to make sure that the Caldwell's spirits understood what she had been trying to do.

She sighed in resignation and started putting the parlor back together again. She lifted the lid on the piano and put the long prop back in place. She stepped around to the keyboard and decided to leave the fallboard closed for the time being. Next, she righted the bench and knelt down to sort through the mess of sheet music on the floor.

She gathered it all up, stuffed it into the benches' compartment, and let the lid close. Then, with a determined expression, she set her shoulders and stalked out to the foyer, intent on yanking that painting off the wall.

No! You mustn't!

The whispered shriek stopped her in her tracks. She watched in the mirror as an older woman stepped timidly into view.

"Mrs. Caldwell?"

"Please, you mustn't. It isn't finished."

Lily glanced at the painting and frowned. "I don't understand. It's framed and hanging on the wall for all to see. Of course, it's finished."

As Lily stepped to the painting and grasped the sides of the frame, the woman in the mirror rushed away.

It isn't finished! It was supposed to be a surprise!

The shriek had just barely finished when another crash sounded from the parlor.

Lily let go of the painting and rushed back into the parlor. The bench had been tipped over again, the sheet music scattered wide.

As Lily righted the bench and began to gather up the sheets of paper, Mrs. Caldwell appeared in the parlor mirror.

"Isn't finished! Supposed to be a surprise!" Mrs. Caldwell shrieked.

Lily again stuffed the sheets into the bench. She slammed the lid and turned to the mirror. "I'm going to get that painting now, no matter what you tip over."

Before Lily could even take a step, the woman was gone from the mirror. The parlor doors slammed shut and the sheet music exploded out of the bench and rained onto the floor.

Surprise! Not finished!

Lily charged to the parlor doors and grasped the handles. She tugged and barely got them open a few inches before they were slammed shut again.

Not finished!

Lily turned to face into the room. "You're clearly intent on my not touching that painting. But really, it *is* finished. It wouldn't be framed and hung if it wasn't."

In response, the fallboard was thrown open and random notes came from the piano, as though someone were pounding on the keys.

Not finished!

Lily was already tired of this game. Lily glared at the woman as she appeared back in the mirror. Daniel seemed to have no trouble communicating with her. "Why can't you just tell me what in the hell you're talking about?"

Accompanied by a shriek, all the sheet music flew into the air. As pages wafted to the floor, they were flung into the air again.

Lily pressed her back against the parlor doors and watched the cascade of papers. "The sheet music.... Do you want me to look at the sheet music?"

The papers all settled to the floor.

Lily gathered them up.

Then she sat on the piano bench with the pile on her lap and sorted through them.

Amongst all the commercially printed sheets, there were some blank sheets of staff paper and three numbered staff pages with pencilled-in notes.

Lily had a hunch. She set them on the music rack in order. She centered herself, lay her hands on the keys and played. It was a haunting, beautiful song but cut off abruptly.

She played it again, growing a bit more familiar with it as she went through it a second time. It still ended in an odd place.

Lily looked at the mirror to find Mrs. Caldwell watching. "It isn't finished, is it?"

Mrs. Caldwell smiled, hesitantly and kept watching her.

Lily put a hand to her chest. "And you want me to finish it?"

Mrs. Caldwell's smile grew wide.

Lily was crestfallen. "I don't... That is to say, I've never... I can play just fine. I've just... I've never written music before."

This time the shriek was more of a wail or moan. Whatever it was, it was not a pleasant sound, and Lily clapped her hands over her ears and shut her eyes until it stopped.

When she opened them again, Mrs. Caldwell was gone.

"She was adamant," Lily told Daniel as she paced back and forth in the parlor. It had been late in the evening before she'd been able to find him in the mirror. "Pretty upset when I explained I'd never written a song before."

"She believes finishing the song is the key to getting everyone out of here," Daniel said. "And that it has to happen by midnight on Halloween."

Lily looked strained. "But that's tonight! How am I going to get that done in..." Lily checked the time on her phone. "... just over two hours?"

Daniel watched her from the mirror. "I think you're focusing on the wrong thing. Just finish the song."

Lily turned toward the mirror and held her arms out, imploring. "How?!"

Daniel shrugged. "Instinct."

"Instinct?"

"You've played a lot of songs, Lily. You used to play with your eyes closed."

"But that was after I'd learned the song."

"My love, we only have two hours left. You've got to try something." He caught and held Lily's gaze for a long moment.

Resigned, Lily strode to the piano and sat on the bench. The three sheets of the half-finished song waited for her. She scanned the notes, looking for the pattern that would allow her to create and play the rest of the song freely.

She set her fingers on the keys and played the first few notes. When she fumbled the next couple, she looked up self-consciously at Daniel in the parlor mirror. She could feel her gut tighten as the minutes ticked by.

She started again, got by the first place she fumbled, only to foul it up again a few notes farther on. Her fingers felt heavy and uncoordinated. Her heart beat heavily in her ears, her hands suddenly clammy over the keys.

She licked her lips, rubbed her palms together and set her hands in place to start again.

"Lily?"

She looked at the mirror.

He smiled. "Do you remember my last birthday? When you played my song despite the fact that everyone was there? You confessed to me later how nervous you were? Do you remember?"

She nodded, suddenly more nervous.

"Close your eyes."

"But – "

"Shhh. Close them."

Lily swallowed thickly, made sure her fingers were where she knew they were, and let her eyes flutter closed.

"I know you can do it," Daniel whispered.

She took a deep breath and let her fingers strike the first notes. And the notes after that. Lily let go of all her doubts and worries, let her mind disengage and let her heart guide her along the bars of the song.

She really was playing by instinct.

When she got to the end of the notes on the page, she just kept going. Kept playing. She let the music carry her up and away, farther and deeper than any song had moved her for a very long while.

When the bright glow penetrated even her eyelids, she dared not open her eyes. She didn't want to break the spell. Instead, she let the music envelope her as the melody built and built, stronger and higher, until she and the music became as one.

Just as she came to the very final, haunting notes, the sound of breaking glass in front of the piano and out in the foyer made her jump. The bright glow faded with the sound of the last note.

In that moment, she knew it had worked. She'd set them all free. She felt the tears streaming down her face at the thought. She didn't dare open her eyes. Seeing the ruined mirrors would confirm her fears.

"Good-bye, Daniel," she whispered before letting the tears overtake her.

She screamed when a hand landed gently on her shoulder.

"Lily?"

When she opened her eyes, there stood Daniel, big as life.

She surged up from the piano bench and into his arms, a sob escaping her.

"Shhh, my love. It's alright. I'm here now and I'm not going anywhere."

After many moments, Lily cleared her throat, kissed him on the cheek and pulled back to look at him. "How?"

Daniel shook his head. "I don't know for sure. Maybe that's what happens when you move from the ethereal plane to the real world?"

Lily looked past him at the rest of the room and all the other people she had freed with her playing, including Mr. and Mrs. Caldwell.

"How are we going to explain the sudden appearance of all of you again?"

Mr. Caldwell held up a hand. "No need. We shan't be here for long."

Mrs. Caldwell smiled. "Your playing was lovely, my dear. Just what we needed. But now, we've been trapped here for far too long. It's really the last place we want to be."

"So, we'll all be out of your hair in an instant. There's just one thing..." Mr. Caldwell strode forward and lifted the portrait of him and his wife off the wall. "We'll take this with us if you don't mind."

"Not at all." Lily turned to Daniel. "We'll have to see if we can get a portrait painted of the new owners of the house."

"That we will, my love. That we will."

Mark Posey was born and raised in Edmonton, Canada. He has worked as a bartender, a gas jockey, an insurance salesman, a house framer, and a cabinet installer. He also had a ten-year career as a professional wrestler. He toured across Canada on the independent wrestling circuit facing such opponents as The Honky Tonk Man, Dan Severn, The British Bulldog Jr., and NWA World Heavyweight Champion Adam Pearce.

When he's not writing, Mark enjoys cooking, woodworking, watching hockey, and scrolling through social media or taking a nap with his three cats: Pippin, Merry, and Strider.

Mark and his wife, author Tracy Cooper-Posey, raised three children: Terry, Matthew, and Katherine and now live in their constantly-under-renovations home in Edmonton.

Mark loves to hear from readers so please feel free to contact him at: mark@markposeyauthor.com, or on https://MarkPoseyAuthor.com

The Werewolf Curse

by Tami Veldura

NARIAH BOYD MARCHED THROUGH THE woods behind her house without her usual cheerfulness. The afternoon was bright, the breeze pleasant, and the birds were singing, but Nariah frowned as she watched her steps over scrabbling rock. Instead of a water bottle, she carried a sturdy stick, and instead of enjoying the afternoon, she threw a concerned look over her shoulder at the man following the trail she broke.

It wasn't often Nariah lead anyone into the woods, let alone Varrien Vicaro, eligible only son of a billionaire. And a werewolf.

Elidee had set Nariah up on a blind date with Varrien a few months ago. Nariah had expected disaster, but Varrien had been a generous date and held a good conversation. It was only afterward Nariah learned of his heir-to-the-business status and she was still figuring out how she felt about that.

To complicate matters, his father was the werewolf equivalent of a king. A pack leader among leaders. The ultimate authority over all werewolves in the western States. Which made Varrien some kind of prince-apparent.

Nariah wasn't sure about that either.

But it was his werewolf-side she needed today. His dating eligibility just made things awkward when Nariah's friend Elidee asked for updates.

Varrien had come dressed in jeans and a polo shirt. Nariah thought the jeans were designer and the button-down polo shirt was certainly fancier than anything she had in her own closet. Despite that, it was the most dressed down she'd ever seen him. Without a suit jacket or anything. He wore a pair of sneakers—she didn't recognize the brand — and while his steps were sure, Nariah suspected this was the most rural experience he'd hand in a long time. He kept twitching at the bugs that droned past his head.

Nariah wore a beat-up pair of hiking boots, a loose pair of pants she'd found on the bargain rack of the local Goodwill, and whatever t-shirt had been on top of the pile in the drawer — a faded NASA logo swirled over some planets. She poked at the overgrown rocks and roots with her staff and kept half an eye out for deer shed.

The back edge of Nariah's small property abutted national park forest. Her cottage sat in the center of a single acre, but suburbia sprawled in every direction. Her neighborhood was urban, but her back yard was as wild as managed forest could get. The park boundaries stretched for miles to the foothills and up into the mountains in the distance. It was a lot of room to get lost in.

Or to find things that should have remained lost.

"Will it still be there?" Varrien asked as they navigated through some close tree trunks. His deep voice had a resonation Nariah hadn't noticed before. Like he belonged in these woods — despite the designer jeans — and the woods recognized his right to be there.

Nariah always felt like a visitor. And she always took care to thank the forest for its hospitality.

"I hope so," Nariah said. "I think."

"You think?" Varrien laughed.

But Nariah frowned again. "A pile of bones that big is weird. A pile that big going missing two days later…?" She shook her head. "I don't think that's better."

"If it walked off, it's not your problem," he said, with the kind of vocal shrug that told Nariah Varrien was used to having problems handled for him.

Nariah blanched at the idea of a six-foot pile of bones sprouting legs and ambling off into the forest like some horrible Baba Yaga. "Something like this always becomes my problem in the end," Nariah muttered.

She'd been on a hike through these woods a few days ago on the lookout for deer shed and any wildlife bones that still held on to their spirits. Nariah could see and interact with spirits of all kinds, but animal spirits were easier to work with. They understood death, decay, and the rebirth cycle better than humans. They were willing to donate their bones to charms and wards that Nariah sold to warn about vampires and harpies. Sometimes the spirits even tagged along, living in their old bones after she'd transformed them into jewelery.

But the bones she'd found hadn't just been a leftover skull or a stray scapula. She'd stumbled over a cache of some kind, a massive pile of deer, hog, and other bones taller than her and capped with a wolf skull on top.

It was the wolf skull that really gave her pause. Nariah had extensive experience with bones from all sorts of animals. Even from a distance, the wolf skull had seemed too large. The jaw too long. The crown too wide at the back.

Nariah knew a wolf skull when she saw one, but she'd never had a chance to study a werewolf skull.

And the pile of bones it sat on top didn't strike her as a welcome invitation to start now.

She'd reached out to Varrien with the very odd request to join her today. She wanted him to confirm the skull belonged to a werewolf, or maybe tell her this kind of cache was the doing of the local pack. She wanted some reassurance.

A six-foot pile of bones in the woods was eerie, even to the Bone Witch. Nariah had never seen anything like it.

She pushed the low branch of a pine aside, holding it clear for Varrien to step up the granite and join her. This rock shelf lay at a slight angle between two ancient pine trees—their gnarled roots had plunged through cracks on the edges, breaking off a boulder the size of a car that had become a ramp up to the top. The stone caused a break in the canopy above, which let a rare spotlight of sunlight hit the forest floor. Blue-eyed grass sprang out of every edge and stone overlap where even a dusting of dirt had lodged, reaching for the sun with tiny five-petal violet flowers. Light green and yellow lichen crusted the rock itself, and a dark stain had spread in the center.

The pile of bones still sat there, unexplained. It didn't make her feel better.

Small vertebra, foot bones, and pieces piled up at the base, like someone had swept them from the nooks and crannies of the rock. Phalanges and remnant bones stacked like cairns. An intact spine, a large deer by the look of it, curled up one side. Its ribs branched outward, hugging a hodgepodge pile of other bits. Some of the ribs had extensions hinged onto them, other ribs, a couple of tusks from the local pig population.

The wolf skull sat on top.

"Weird," Varrien said as he stepped carefully around the pile. His steps remained cautiously clear of that dark stain on the stone. Dappled sunlight shifted across the pile with the breeze.

"I thought bones were white," Varrien said, his voice speculative. "These are all..."

"Fresh," said Nariah. "They're still greasy from the bodies they lived in, and that spine is only holding together thanks to some tendons still in place. Bones don't really connect otherwise." That was probably the source of the stain, too. Old fluids seeping out of the bones. Marrow and oils.

Varrien wrinkled his nose and stepped away from circling the pile. "Ew," he said. Then he sniffed. "Shouldn't it stink, then?"

He was right. It should have. Nariah sniffed cautiously, then stooped closer to sniff again when she noticed no sour, rotting smell. Not even that touch of sweet-ness that came with old meat. Nothing at all. She peered at the pile, between the crossed leg bones and tangled pelvises. No flies. No beetles or grubs. Her gut tightened. No natural pile of bones would be this untouched.

No bones would be in a pile like this naturally, of course, she was just hoping Varrien had an explanation that didn't lead directly to a necromancer hiding in her forest.

"Is the skull a werewolf?" she asked.

Varrien looked up at the pile. It was overhead for him and Nariah only stood at his shoulder. "I dunno," he said with a shrug. "Are werewolf skulls different from wolf skulls?" Nariah shot him a flat look and he chuckled. "Sorry, just poking fun. I'll need a closer look."

Before she could stop him — before Nariah even real-ized what he was going to do — Varrien wedged a sneaker into the pile and stepped up, reaching his long arms over the spine to grab the skull on top.

His fingers wrapped around the muzzle. When he yanked it free, the bottom jaw and several feet of spine came with it. A lot more spine than a wolf would have and, now that it was unwinding from the pile like a wrapped extension cord, a lot more spine than a deer, too.

"Oh my goddess, you can't just pick up random bones from the spooky pile in the forest," Nariah hissed.

"Why, are they cursed?" He shot her a wry grin, just a flash of one sharp canine tooth, as he turned the skull over in his hands. He flipped it upside down. The lower jaw snapped closed, its teeth perfectly aligned. Nariah watched him stretch the fingers of his hand between the protruding angular processes in the back of the jaw. They were so wide, he barely reached them between thumb and pinky finger. He turned the skull over again, peering at the spot where the assembled deer spine connected to the rympanic bulb. Did he know the scientific anatomy? Nariah had an entire library worth of books, diagrams, and research back at the house to help her identify and re-assemble a skeleton.

"This is the tell," he said, turning the back of the skull to face her. The spinal cord swung down past his hip. "The ridge here above the occipital lobe." He ran his finger across the bone in question, skimming down the back. "It's a soft point in a natural wolf. Not this ridge. We have a lot more muscle back here — higher bite force — and this bone ridge is where all those muscles attach." He rotated the skull until her eyes met his through the hole made by the wide cheekbone. "The zygomatic arch is wider to accom-modate, but that's not always so obvious."

He offered her the skull. "Have a look."

Nariah pursed her lips. This wasn't how she preferred to engage with the forest's bones. When she found some-thing in the underbrush there was a process. A way to ask permission, check for spirits, and clear any lingering malaise. It was a slow, respectful approach. Nariah had a relationship with these woods she didn't want to disrupt.

But if anything had been tied to these bones, she would have felt it by now, surely. She stretched her spiri-tual sense over the skull and pile, but it just sat there, inert. And weirdly bug-free.

She reached for the skull.

And the moment Varrien dropped it into her palm she realized her mistake.

It wasn't inert, it was asleep. Spiritual power surged out of Nariah's palm and into the skull. It traveled up the spine in a wave of ghostly blue. The bone pile drew on her like a battery, draining her dry of spirit energy in only two or three heartbeats. She only had time to gasp softly as she sank to her knees with sudden exhaustion.

Wrapped around Nariah's wrist, a bracelet of pol-ished white bone sprang to life. A snake spirit, pale blue and mostly transparent, slid out of her spine bones and coiled on Nariah's wrist. She struck the wolf skull with force, all fangs bare, and while she passed through the physical bone, her attack hit the spiritual.

The skull toppled from Nariah's hand. Her energy stabilized immediately. She threw herself back from the pile, stumbling up to her feet on the granite, and grabbed Varrien's arm to drag him along with her. He helped her stay upright. Nariah's snake dropped off her wrist and coiled on the granite in front of her, a defender the size of a tennis ball.

"What the hell was that?" Varrien asked. He ran a hand up the back of her arm.

Nariah could only point at the bone pile.

Nariah's shot of energy had given it some kind of jumpstart. She could feel the spiritual being drawn to it, pulled in gently from distant corners of the forest. *She* felt drawn to it, a subtle pull that hadn't been there before.

Her snake fed off the passing power, sipping at it, flinging her ghostly tongue into the stream. She grew from the size of a garter snake to a rattler, broad in the body and far more deadly. She kept sipping as the incoming power picked up speed. She stole drops of it as it passed by.

The bone pile didn't react at first. Nariah pulled Varrien away to the edge of the granite shelf, her eyes wide. The ambient power picked up speed, swirling as it hit the bones and was absorbed into something Nariah couldn't identify.

"That's not good," she said.

Varrien glanced at the bones and back to her. "Explain," he demanded, his voice clipped.

She swallowed, her throat dry. "It took my power when I touched it to bootstrap itself. It's collecting more power." She pointed at the fallen skull, its teeth agape and empty eye socket laughing at her from the stone. "Grab the skull and rip it off."

Varrien moved to do as she bid. He didn't question her, just stooped to grasp the skull with one hand, the constructed spine with the other, and yanked the two apart with every muscle in his body.

Spirit power flashed in Nariah's vision. The skull didn't just remain attached, it suddenly lurched upward on its own, yanking out of Varrien's hands and retracting to the top of the bone pile.

Varrien didn't need Nariah's cry of warning to jump back and put distance between himself and the pile. A spike of bone—clustered boar tusks—thrust into the space he'd been, retracting slowly when it missed.

Nariah got the impression the nascent spirit was toying with them.

Because something was certainly growing inside those bones. A gathering was happening, like something old waking up after a long and cold hibernation. Only this thing wasn't a natural spirit. Pieces of it developed from boar tusk and territory fights. Others from deer fleeing through the woods. And on top, a wolf. A predator who woke faster and stronger than the others, controlling them all from the skull above.

Two spirit flames, bright blue and fierce, sprang to life in the werewolf skull's eyes. It wasn't life. It was an echo. A strong one.

It assembled itself. Nariah couldn't explain how else the shape of a creature unfolded from the pile. Bones shifted against each other, attached in unnatural ways, and with the power of ghostly blue spirit, lifted a monster onto four legs and a tail. It was nominally a wolf, but the tail had been assembled from spine, ribs, and tusks. It had a cluster of spikes at the end like some kind of dinosaur. The legs weren't just radius and ulna, but a dozen radiuses and ulnas wrapped around each other like woven vines, terminating in claws the size of swords stolen from ribs.

Tiny phalanges, hoofs, and lumpy sesamoid bones clustered around joints and filled in gaps where they didn't belong. They moved around by themselves, dragged into place by bands of blue power that wrapped the entire construct in muscle-like fibers. The wolf skull was subsumed back to front by overlapping bones that shifted into a larger wolf head. Bone shards and bits fell together to mimic the rough fur around the neck and shoulders.

It stood nine feet tall, at least.

Between Nariah and the bone wolf, her spirit snake rose up like a cobra. Power had lent her strength and size. Now she resembled an anaconda more than a garter snake—a huge titian boa forty feet long and so fat around the middle Nariah would be hard-pressed to hug her and meet her hands on the other side.

She hissed at the wolf, her dark blue fangs dense with power and glittering with threat. The creature turned its spirit-flame eyes on her.

Nariah shoved Varrien off the rock. He fell, managed to twist and catch himself on all fours in the pine needles. Nariah followed. She landed heavily without Varrin's wolf-grace and staggered to keep her feet.

Nariah's snake hissed again, her body coiling side to side on the stone. Nariah could feel the power in her. How it cycled in her cord-like body, ready to attack. She was thick with it, more blue than transparent. Almost solid. Big enough to pose a threat the bone wolf couldn't ignore.

The snake struck. She lashed forward suddenly, fangs first, and hit the wolf's shoulder. Her spirit fangs sank through bone without any resistance. It was the spirit holding the construct together that shuddeed under her assault. She pulled back. Some of the intensity in her fangs had faded.

Nariah sensed the spirit injection her snake had made, the way it twisted inside the wolf. For a moment

103

her hope soared — perhaps, through her snake, Nariah could take over the construct and command it to stand down.

But the spirit venom was spread too thin. Nariah sensed the moment it failed to infect the wolf and was instead integrated into its own power. They'd just made it stronger.

The wolf shook itself. It growled — the sound of grinding bones twisting against each other.

Varrien grabbed Nariah's arm, his grip hard. "Run. I'll hold it off —"

"Run and do what?" She snapped at him. "Do you have someone who can help?"

The way his face paled told Nariah everything she needed to know. "Me," she said, "I'm the person that helps when it comes to this shit."

Varrien's lips pressed into a tight line. "Okay," he said, voice tight. "What's the play?"

"We need to disassemble it somehow."

"I couldn't yank the skull off," he said.

"The bones are being held together with power —" Nariah was cut short as the wolf lunged for her snake. It slid through most of the spirit, rib-claws scratching furrows in the stone.

Nariah and Varrin ducked as the wolf's spiked tail swung overhead. It crashed into a pine tree and lodged there, boar tusk sunk deep into the wood. It heaved against the tree. Pine needles rained downward. Nariah slipped around the stone shelf, but Varrien moved in.

He grabbed one of the tail spikes not stuck in a tree. It slid out of the bone construct without any effort, but Nariah could see the strings of gossamer blue power that kept it connected to the whole. When Varrien chucked the tusk into the woods with all of his strength, it swung like a boomerang around a cluster of trees and right back to the bone wolf. The tusk smacked into the wolf's tail and slid down into the cluster, back into place.

"Shit," Varrien barked. "What was that?"

The wolf yanked its tail free and, thankfully, didn't spare them a glance. Nariah's snake held its attention.

"New plan: bring me a bone."

"Did you just ask me to fetch?" Varrien flashed a smile at her as he scrambled up the stone. He let the spiky tail swing overhead as the wolf swiped claws at Nariah's snake. With deft fingers he yanked another bone free—possibly a deer leg bone, but it was sheared off into a deadly point—and held tight as he brought it back.

Nariah wrapped her hands around the bone and Varrin's grip. She reached for the magic tying it to the wolf and snapped the strands easily. The bone itself seemed to dim. Nariah pulled Varrien to the side—just in case the bone wanted to stab someone—and let it drop.

It hit the pine needles and rolled onto its side,

Inert.

"Right," Nariah said. "One down, nine hundred to go."

Bones rolled against each other. Grinding. Growling. The wolf turned on the granite shelf to face them both, blue fire eyes ablaze. It looked at the inert leg bone at Nariah's feet, then back up to her. It snarled.

"He didn't like that," Varrien said helpfully.

"How do you know it's male."

"I get a vibe." Varrien shrugged.

They split, diving to either side as the construct dove off the shelf with teeth agape. Nariah swung herself around the trunk of a pine, high-stepping over roots and bushes, only to realize the construct wasn't after either of them. It had landed on the bone they stole and pawed at it. To Nariah's surprise, it grasped the fragment with its teeth and gulped the thing down whole.

And a familiar bone shard sprouted from the wolf's tail, once more reattached by spirit power.

"Shit. Shit." Nariah cursed as she slipped further around the stone shelf. She ducked low, eventually meeting up with Varrien around the other side.

"What was that shit?" he asked. "We can't disassemble it if it just reabsorbs the bones!"

"I know, I know." Nariah put her back to a thick tree and let out a shuddering breath of nerves. She started speaking out loud, trying to focus on what they knew, looking for a solution. "We can take bones, but we have to sever the connection. It can re-establish the connection, but it has to be in contact to do that."

Varrien leaned around the tree to check on the construct, his shoulder close to hers. "Maybe your snake can run away with them?" He thought out loud. "But how do we do that more than once or twice?"

"The snake!" Nariah wrapped one hand around her snake-spine bracelet and closed her eyes to focus. "We need to give those bones to someone else so the wolf can't reclaim them." She sent the shape of the idea down her spiritual connection and felt the snake coil in agreement. She would claim the bones.

Nariah drew on her power and felt the chill of it sweep away her nerves. She straightened.

"Whoa. Your eyes are glowing blue."

Her power danced on her skin. Nariah spoke with the voices of the spirits of the forest, resonant and old. "Bring us the bones."

On the stone shelf, the spirit snake struck twice, hard. She drove the wolf construct back and lunged up overhead. The wolf's back leg slipped off the shelf and he scrambled to regain his footing. In the chaos, Varrien grabbed a handful of bones: some hooves, a short leg bone, a handful of spine pieces from a raccoon, perhaps. Tiny.

Nariah lay her hands over his and snapped the threads that bound the bones to the wolf, as before. She heard him snarl in response. He knew. With a push of power, Nariah wrapped the bones in the spirit of her snake. She drew the threads of it from the spine bracelet on her wrist and the snake accepted the pieces. The bones dimmed when the wolf's power was severed. They glowed again when the snake took possession of them.

Nariah lifted her hands. Varrien opened his. The little bones flung themselves into the air on strings of power and zipped right past the wolf. He tried to snap his teeth at them, but they dodged and spun away. Each bone sank into the semi-transparent snake. They hit the surface and slowed abruptly, like falling through water. Or Jell-o. The snake flexed around each bone, pushing them up her body where, like the wolf, they assembled themselves into a mask around her eyes.

Fire burst to life there, her gaze suddenly as sharp as her fangs.

The wolf roared. His bone fur shuddered and rattled, and his eyes flared with fury.

"Okay, now we've really pissed him off," Varrien said.

"Because it worked." Nariah pointed at her snake's head. "We claimed the bones and he can't take them back."

Varrien nodded, his gaze sharp. "Just nine hundred more to go," he said wryly.

He dove back into the fight, relying on Nariah's snake to keep the wolf occupied. There wasn't much Nariah could do to help him. She wasn't as fast or agile. She couldn't slide under the wolf's tail like stealing home base and snag rib-spikes as she went.

But she snapped the threads of power when he returned and established new ones with her snake. The ribs flew through the air and sank into her snake's blue body. All of them rushed to her head, where she assembled a mouth full of bone-fangs and used them immediately. She coiled. Lunged. And blue sparks flared where her fangs struck shoulder and leg. Bone fragments went flying. The wolf was pushed back off the shelf once more.

Varrien was there, prepared to yank more bones from the wolf's tail. The snake kept the pressure on, pulling bones out of place now that she had the fangs to bite with. Like the wolf, she swallowed them whole, replacing the spirit animating them with her own.

Varrien returned to Nariah with a scapula and the femur of something large. Moose, perhaps. The wolf turned on them, furious now that he was being picked off from both directions. Nariah grabbed Varrien's hands and yanked him forward, pulling them both around a tree just as the wolf's claws raked the air. He struck the trunk, throwing wood splinters and fragments everywhere.

Nariah severed the bones in Varrien's hands and took them. "Split up!" she yelled over the sound of grinding bone.

Varrien ducked into the surrounding forest immediately. Nariah spun away the other direction. She tied the bones to her snake. She paused only long enough to wind her arm back and chuck them both toward the spirit on the shelf. The scapula soared like a single-wing copter, spinning on its own off-center mass.

The wolf surged for Nariah.

The femur nailed the wolf right in the forehead, bounced off, and twirled to the snake.

The wolf reared back in alarm. Nariah took the chance to run. She heard the wolf's bone-grinding snarl behind her, but didn't risk looking back. It would only slow her down, and these tree roots were just asking for a twisted ankle.

She squeezed between two narrow trees and took hard right back toward the stone shelf. The bone wolf piled up on the trees behind her, like a bag of bones thrown into a wall.

Nariah vaulted up onto the stone slab and jumped over the coiled body of her snake. There were a bunch of loose bones floating around in her now. Spine pieces, ribs, tusks, hooves. The scapula had been positioned like a nose-horn, the small bones acting like a shifting face, and enough spine stretched from the back of the head to give her a real spooky look.

Varrien leapt up onto the shelf from the back. His arms were full of long bones—legs and a few antlers.

"I have more—"

The snake twisted and ate Varrien whole. Her head slammed down over him—he squealed in alarm—and slowly pulled back upward as the stolen bones reassembled to leave the werewolf standing there wide-eyed and arms empty.

The new bones took their positions in the snake's body.

Varrien blinked at Nariah, then wrinkled his nose and said, "I feel rather sullied."

"Did she hurt you?"

"No, I'll just need therapy for years," he quipped.

"I know a guy," Nariah said, her smile sly.

They turned to face the wolf as he clambered back up onto the slab.

He was noticeably smaller, now. A good third of his bones had been stolen, much of his tail reduced to a stub, and he stood shorter than before. His bones had rearranged to keep him stocky and strong, if only six feet tall instead of nine.

Varrien spread his feet and growled under his breath, "Second verse. Same as the first." And with only a puff of dirt and pine needles, he vanished again into the woods.

The wolf snarled at Nariah and her snake. It prowled to one side, grinding its bones, and glaring. Nariah saw it flick a bone ear—another scapula—toward the forest, likely tracking Varrien's movements.

109

Nariah's snake coiled in herself and hissed in response. Her little bones rattled against each other.

When the wolf lunged for Nariah, her snake had enough bones to intercept the attack entirely. She wrapped herself around the wolf's foreleg, coiled around its neck, and constricted. There wasn't any breath in the wolf to choke the life out of, but physical constriction still worked.

The wolf crashed onto one immobile shoulder. Nariah dove in close at the wolf's back where struggling claws couldn't reach her. She started yanking bones out of the spine two-handed. She sliced through the strings of spirit holding them and threw bones by the handful at her snake. She pulled out any bone she could reach, aiming to reduce the construct's mass as quickly as possible. There didn't seem to be a heart or lungs—not even bone-amalgams of them—to cripple the creature. Only pieces.

The pieces began to twist. Nariah slipped away and dropped off the shelf. Since the wolf couldn't break the snake's hold, he decided to slip out instead, reassembling bones from a collapse of cohesion back into his wolf-form.

The snake gulped a mouthful of ribs down in the process.

Then they faced each other on the stone shelf, hissing and growling—evenly matched for size.

Varrien struck next. He waited for the snake to engage again—she attacked fangs out and hissing—before he slid into the melee.

His speed was incredible. Nariah couldn't track his movements, only the moments where he slowed down enough to throw bones at Nariah's snake. He slipped around the back of the wolf, picking bones out of the tail and rear legs.

He seemed to fade easily away from the construct's claws and never tried to take a hit just to grab another bone.

But fewer bones somehow lent the construct more speed. Maybe it could apply more power to less mass. Or perhaps it was getting desperate. In a sudden turn, the bone-wolf inverted itself—head became tail in the blink of an eye—and claws scythed through the air from a new direction.

Varrien went flying. He crashed onto the edge of the stone shelf and slid right off the edge, limp.

Nariah screamed. Her heart and stomach both plummeted off the shelf with him and vanished.

Her snake surged in to coil around the wolf again and restrain it, but the snake only managed to secure a rear leg. The wolf severed its own bones to escape. It wouldn't allow the snake to wrap around it a second time.

Nariah scrambled through the forest and slid to her knees at Varrien's shoulder. He was already groaning and half-awake, thank the Goddess, one hand in the pine needles to lever himself upward, the other against his head.

"Oh, my goddess, what's broken? How bad is it?" Nariah hovered her hands over his chest and arms, hesitating to grab anything in case she caused more problems.

"I'm fine," he said, and immediately clutched at his ribs with a hiss.

Nariah inched closer, looking for blood or bones. "Don't lie to m—!"

Varrien flung his arm around Nariah's waist and rolled them both over in the needles. Grinding bone and a vibrating impact hit the dirt where he'd been. The wolf snarled in Nariah's ear, and she shrieked. Fear forced her to curl up against Varrien's chest.

Her snake sent a spike of alarm, a desperate twist of warning through their spirit bomb.

Despite the fear, Nariah got one arm free and threw her power at the wolf through the palm of her hand over Varrien's shoulder. She screamed the whole time, half in terror, half in pain as she channeled raw magic directly into the open mouth of the beast descending on them.

Bones fell apart. They rained down over Varrien's back—all the modified teeth, tiny fur bones, even the mask around the eyes. The blue fire winked out.

And Nariah's snake had enough time to sweep off the shelf and reassemble her bones into a wide cobra hood between Varrien and the wolf. She claimed the fallen bones, bulking her shape with new plate armor and spikes. Longer fangs. More deadly than ever.

The wolf staggered back from Nariah's blast, disoriented and depleted. The snake pressed her advantage. She drove the wolf back, stole the last of his extra bones, and coiled around the core left behind—a werewolf skeleton with barely enough spirit left to animate itself.

Nariah pushed Varrien's arms open. She gained her feet, but stumbled against a tree, suddenly dizzy. Pushing through it was a bad idea, she could feel her muscles fatiguing. Everything in her wanted nothing more than to lay down and sleep for a year to recover. Shoving power into the air like that had torn up more than the wolf.

She lurched toward her snake and the remnent wolf spirit anyway.

Her legs gave the second she committed. A curved tail made of smooth bone caught her and she wrapped her arms around it. Varrien appeared behind her. He slung one arm over his shoulder and tugged her close by the hip.

"What do you need?" He held her steady.

"Contact," Nariah gasped.

Varrien walked them both closer. The wolf growled and snapped its teeth. The skeleton was still animated, even if the fire eyes were gone. Nariah slipped her hand between snake coils and gripped a vertebrae. Feeling the spirit directly was a shock. It was so small compared to the construct they had fought. And furious.

The spirit's anger overwhelmed her at first touch, and she lost herself. Like being swamped by a wave at the

112

beach. She had to struggle back to the surface and she didn't have any spiritual energy to spare.

Her snake's spirit remained strong, though, and she lifted Nariah back to herself gently. Nariah took a gasping breath.

She slipped her other arm off Varrien's shoulders and leaned against the snake to get both hands on the wolf. This time she was prepared for the fury it tried to throw at her. She let it slip past.

And only then could she see the wolf wasn't angry at her, but at being bound. The skeleton was a werewolf and the spirit was a werewolf, but the two didn't match. These weren't this spirit's bones and it raged against the cage they made.

It was a simple thing to release it.

Nariah severed the spirit's ties to these bones and gave it a nudge. The skeleton collapsed into a pile of separate bones, tumbling over Nariah's hands and onto the ground with a clatter. She sensed the werewolf linger only for a moment. Just a breath, where he touched Nariah's spirit in thanks. She could feel his relief.

Then he was gone.

Nariah accepted Varrien's help to stand up and back away. Her snake uncoiled, then with deliberate care, she began to drop her stolen bones into a pile on the forest floor.

"It's done, then?"

"Yes. The spirit is gone." Although, not every spirit in the woods had left. Nariah let Varrien sit her down on a rock. She pulled him down to sit with her and pointed at the growing pile of bones. "Watch," she said.

She could see the ghosts who laid claim to these bones. They wavered between the trees, cautious of the snake's outsized power. But they had sensed the werewolf leave like Nariah had. They knew the fight was done.

Nariah's snake shrunk down as she lost the borrowed bones. From a massive ten foot tall titian boa down to

python, rattlesnake, and finally, garter snake. The little gar-
den-snake Nariah had found in her yard all those years ago.
She glowed bright blue with condensed spirit power and
when Nariah bent low and offered her the bracelet made
from her own spine, the snake slipped back inside her own
bones with a spiritual sigh that echoed in the trees.

The forest spirits approached. A hog, first, with a cluster of little hoglets trailing behind her. She rooted through
the bones and claimed hers: spine, skull, radius and ulna,
hooves, tusks, pelvis and femur, all the little bones in the
feet. She snuffled through the pile for her hoglets' bones,
nosing them one by one into each tumbling baby ghost.
Mother hog assembled her bones in a proper skeletal ar-
mature of a hog, the babies were less defined, and happy
to swap bones among themselves when the mood struck
them.

Only after the little family had found every last tooth
did they trot silently back into the trees — a little line of
skeletons snorting and squealing with joy.

Two deer approached next, a doe and her stag. They
pulled long leg bones and an entire rope of spine pieces
out of the pile. They sifted through until the doe found
most of her skeleton. She tossed her head in Nariah's direction and ran off. Nariah liked to think it was a thank you.

A big male boar came crashing through the brush —
passing right through trees and saplings both. He rum-
maged through the bones, finding what was left of his
own, and filling in gaps with some that were left un-
claimed.

The buck pawed at the pile and assigned himself a
huge pair of antlers that had once belonged to a moose.
He pulled additional bones from the pile to reinforce his
legs and torso until he looked like a deer-shaped tank of
bone.

The boar did the same, claiming extra tusks and
hooves and ribs until his spirit was stretched thin with

holding them. He reluctantly put a few tusks back in the pile.

Nariah chuckled. the boar snorted at her, then kicked his back legs and scrambled into the trees. The big deer turned toward the granite shelf and leapt gracefully up onto the stone. His hooves clicked on the rock, and he paused for a moment in the sunlight where Nariah couldn't quite see his spirit anymore, only the bones he animated.

Then with a silent leap off the other side, he was gone.

"There are a bunch of pieces left," Varrien noted. "What happens to them?'

"Their spirits were either gone before the bones were collected, or they were dismissed. Maybe consumed by the wolf. They can be left here to decay naturally," Nariah pushed herself to her feet. "Although I do like the look of that deer pelvis," she said, and pointed to an intact bone on the edge of the remains.

Varrien didn't hesitate to scoop it up, hooking his fingers through the hole of the hip. He offered his arm for Nariah to lean on, but she waved him off.

"I can walk," she said. "It'll just be a slow return."

"'Lead the way."

Nariah gave the stone shelf and the trees a final glance, reaching as far as she dared with her spirit senses to check for anything out of place. Power was weak here after all the turmoil, but it would recover with time. And she found no traces of the werewolf or its anger.

She offered a smile to the wolf skull on the pine needles. Its toothy grin struck her as joyful, now.

Good. It deserved to rest well.

She turned away and lead Varrien back toward home.

"So how does a pile of bones animate in the middle of a forest?" Varrien asked.

Nariah sighed. She turned to glare at him. "'I can't even have five minutes to bask?"

He laughed and held up both hands, the deer pelvis hooked on his thumb. "Right, sorry. You get at least an hour."

"Oh, thank you ever so much."

She rolled her eyes and turned toward home.

TAMI VELDURA IS AN enby/aro/ace author of queer fiction. They have published short stories in anthologies *Fresh Starts, Hauntings, Love Among The Thorns, Love Is Like A Box Of Chocolates, Street Magic* (a Diamond Quill Book Of The Year winner), the magazine *Galaxy's Edge*, and they are a contributing member of the scifi magazine *Boundary Shock Quarterly*. They publish new work every month, crossing every genre, but always featuring queer characters and found families.

Tami's stories often feature a motley crew or an underdog, they often write about chosen family, and even if it's scifi, they always try to squeeze a dragon in. Find out more about Tami at https://tamiveldura.com/ and for more of the Bone Witch, see https://books2read.com/u/m2dvKk.

Did you enjoy this anthology?

How to make a big difference!

Reviews are *powerful*.

Authors and publishers like us, without the financial muscle of a sleek New York publisher backing us, can't take advertisements out in the subways and billboards of the world.

Honest reviews of our books help bring them to the attention of other readers. If you enjoyed this anthology we would be grateful if you could spend just a few minutes leaving a review (it can be as short as you like) on the book's page where you bought it.

Thank you so much!

The Authors and Stories Rule Press

This is a Stories Rule Press title

https://StoriesRulePress.com

www.ingramcontent.com/pod-product-compliance
Lightning Source LLC
Chambersburg PA
CBHW051145020726
47501CB00005B/1681